Graeme J Greenan

Copyright

Copyright © 2018 by Graeme J Greenan

All rights reserved. No part of this book may be reproduced or used in any manner without written permission of the copyright owner except for the use of quotations in a book review.

ISBN: 9781790896387

Contents

Chapter One – The Clearing 5
Chapter Two – Death in the Great Forest 11
Chapter Three – The Riverbank 30
Chapter Four – Return of an Exile 41
Chapter Five – Diplomacy 51
Chapter Six – Bacon, Eggs, and Fractured Memories 69
Chapter Seven – The Wolf and the Tribesman 78
Chapter Eight – Royal Wine and Dragon Root 93
Chapter Nine – Lord Cunningham's Keep 103
Chapter Ten – Sparring Practice 118
Chapter Eleven – The Temple 134
Chapter Twelve – Grace 144
Chapter Thirteen – A Fight Amongst the Ruins 161
Chapter Fourteen – A Taste of One's Own Medicine 176
Chapter Fifteen – The Last Knight of the Hour 186
Chapter Sixteen – Summons 195
Chapter Seventeen – Reprimanded 204
Chapter Eighteen – Roth 218
Epilogue – 235
Acknowledgements – 242

For Karina and Millie
For all your love and encouragement

Chapter One - The Clearing

The night was still; as quiet as the grave. Apart from the occasional chirp from a cricket or call of a nocturnal bird, it could be mistaken for being uninhabited.

The moon was full, its light never failing to find gaps in the thick canopy above, spilling streams of light onto the soft undergrowth. It gave the great forest an eerie, if not haunted opacity. It was both comforting and disturbing at the same time.

Captain Argon enjoyed the feeling of separation it gave him from the teeming masses converged within the towns and cities. He tried to stay away from it, but it was unavoidable – choosing to venture through their shit-stained streets at night where the noise and the accumulation of people were at a minimum. But even then, it grated on his nerves.

The forest itself had many roads and paths coursing through it linking the realm together like veins between arteries. The traders and travellers that traversed them rarely strayed into the deeper parts of the woods through fear of getting lost and never finding their way back to civilisation. Over the years he'd come across more than a few bodies in various stages of decomposition. He never felt any empathy towards them – being almost devoid of the emotion himself.

It was their own fault. Merely nature's way of disposing of the weak and the unable.

Argon had no such problems with the forest. He wasn't arrogant enough to boast he knew it like the back of his hand, but he wasn't far off the mark.

He called his men to a halt, holding a mailed fist in the air as a signal. The men stopped unquestioningly at the command from their leader. He tilted his chin up, taking a deep breath through his nostrils. The air had the thick aroma of foliage, but there was something else. Something he was looking for. Smoke. They were close.

He took in each of his men. They were barely visible, their black armour fashioned in such a way to aid in stealth at night. He grinned wryly and moved forward, his men quickly following suit.

They travelled in silence for another hour. It was slow going, but they weren't in a great rush and Argon enjoyed the wilderness. Their target would have no idea what was coming for him. It had started to rain lightly, the drops pattering against the leaves above their heads. Every so often he would lean his head back to face the downpour and let it wash over his face refreshing him.

The trees and undergrowth began to thin out as they drew closer to a small clearing cut into the forest. The odd stump or two still remained, scattered here and there. At its centre lay a small cottage with a barn adjoined to its northerly side. The bricks were covered in a thick moss which told Argon it must have been built well before he or even his father had been born – not that he knew his father. An axe lay next to a neat pile of firewood in front of the barn.

He looked up at its haphazard, but sturdy looking roof. Plumes of faint, bluish smoke billowed out from it seeming to reach for the sky above like gnarled misshapen claws. Argon smiled a wide toothy grin that was anything but pleasant.

Their target was home.

He'd had a rough idea where the clearing was after they had moored their boat a couple of miles back. His educated guesswork had proved true the second he'd detected a hint of the chimney-smoke in the air.

He knelt down and grasped a handful of leaves and soil. His gauntlet glowed as the mixture caught fire and turned to dust. He had waited a long time for this moment to come. He wanted to savour every second of it.

It would begin here.

There were thirteen of them – including himself. The number was no accident. He chuckled, rising to his feet. He'd take any omen on offer. He nodded to Fargus – his second in command – who approached. "Assign two to each side of the structure. Approach with caution. They know who resides within this tiny little hovel," he said, pointing at the cottage. "Once they have placed the pots of sand, they will retreat back to a safe distance and surround the building. I will ignite them. After that, the roof should collapse in on itself."

Fargus nodded his ascent at his captain's orders. "Survivors, Captain? Other than the target?" he asked.

Argon presumed Fargus knew what the answer would be, but appreciated the man's attention to detail. He was a good soldier, always respecting the line of command with an unwavering loyalty that was a rare thing. He'd never let Argon down.

Argon smiled at his subordinate. "Let me deal with any who survive." He looked towards the cottage, a glint in his eye. "I'm counting on it."

Fargus nodded and moved off to dispense his orders. He watched patiently as eight of his men slowly surrounded the cottage. The remaining soldiers stood behind him, unmoving. They carried satchels containing pots of fire-sand; a highly flammable powder made by the Watalla tribe from the mountains.

The soldiers removed them and slowly approached each corner of the cottage; their lightweight armour and the soft damp ground masking their approach. If Argon closed his eyes, he wouldn't think there was anyone anywhere near him.

Once placed, they withdrew and settled their gaze to their leader. Argon remained still. He took the moment to reflect on the true meaning of what he was about to start. This was the final obstacle. After their target was destroyed, there wouldn't be any more of them to stop what was coming.

He let his anger flow through him. It was like a dam finally breaking its banks, filling him with purpose. He concentrated all of his energy into his fist. It began to glow, red at first, then turned a white so brilliant his men had to turn away lest they be blinded.

He raised his arm, aiming it towards the cottage, and opened his hand releasing all his power. A steady beam of light struck the first pot. He quickly concentrated his power to arc to each of the other containers. They caught fire quickly. Each pot exploded, bathing the clearing in so much light for a moment even Argon forgot it was night.

He sensed the soldiers turning away from the glare, holding their hands up to their faces to shield their eyes. Even from this distance, he could feel the heat of it as brick, mortar, and stone burned and blew apart in all directions – some landing mere feet from where he stood.

The violence of it was simply beautiful, he thought. It was in these moments he truly felt alive. His heart hammered in his chest; a feeling of pure ecstasy.

Within seconds, the roof collapsed. He thought he could hear a scream, he couldn't be sure, the roar was deafening.

He cut the power off like a tap. He was panting from the effort. He bent over, feeling the sweat drip from his forehead to the soft ground. He forgot how much of a toll it took on him. He took a moment to steady his breathing, taking deep breaths and allowed his body to slowly relax. It was why he only used it if there was no other way.

He could hear the muted drone of Fargus' voice as he tried to say something to him. The ringing in his ears made it difficult for him to make out anything discernible. He raised himself up and asked him to repeat what he'd said.

"I said there's at least one survivor, sir." Fargus shouted.

Argon smiled and drew his sword. "Well we can't be rude, Fargus," he said, striding past his second in command. "Let's say hello."

Chapter Two - Death in the Great Forest

Lana kept her distance. She stooped down, wincing at the sound her knees made as they cracked audibly. The wolf she'd been stalking for the last couple of hours had stopped by a small stream. She remained as still as a statue. She dare not move as she'd lost it twice already and was surprised she'd been able to pick up it's trail each time which made her feel as though the wolf had known of her presence from the start and was just toying with her. It was not a comforting thought.

She glanced back in the direction of home. Her father would kill her if he knew she was out alone after dark hunting a wolf. Kneeling in the gloom, she smiled at the idea she'd rather take her chances with the wolf than the scolding her father would dispense if he knew where she was.

He was a good man and she loved him dearly, as a daughter loved a father, but he could be a little overprotective at times. He could still treat her like a little girl. She was nineteen, and after growing up in the woods, learning how to live off the land by her father – the irony wasn't lost on her – she felt she was sometimes treated like some mollycoddled nitwit from the cities.

She waited patiently as the wolf quenched its thirst; its tongue flicked up and down as it drank its fill. Its muzzle dripped with cool stream water making Lana's mouth water a little. She couldn't remember when she'd last taken a drink from her water-skin. Deciding she would sate her thirst after she dealt with the beast, she slowly reached behind her back and pulled an arrow from her quiver.

The moon was bright tonight, making it a lot harder to remain unseen. She didn't want to get too close for two reasons: the first being her quarry, with its sensitive sense of smell, would be able to pick up her scent. The gentle breeze that seemed to always be at her back had caused her much frustration during her hunt. The second, and more important reason of all, was that it was a wolf that weighed three times her bodyweight and had teeth that could strip the flesh from her throat.

She froze as one of the wolf's ears pricked up in her direction. It was quickly followed by a deep, low growl. She cursed. She would need to be quick.

She didn't have a problem with wolves in general – if they kept themselves to themselves. This particular wolf had been venturing further down from the mountains than they were known to do. Down to the villages by the river. The closest village had recently lost twelve sheep, two cows, and countless chickens. A farmer's stable-boy was missing two fingers on his left hand, having lost them protecting his employer's horses. The boy was lucky his father and uncle had found him when they did. They'd chased the wolf back towards the forest before it could cause any more damage.

During her hunt, the one thing that kept playing on her mind was the fact the wolf was alone. Where was its pack? Amidst the accounts and sightings from the villagers, not one of them had mentioned a pack, only that one large beast had been terrorizing their livestock. She shivered as she hoped if there was a pack, it didn't choose this moment to show itself.

She slowly knocked her bow and took aim. The wolf, aware of her presence she did not doubt, turned towards her snarling; it's teeth a brilliant white dripping with a mixture of drool and stream water. Its yellow eyes bored into her with primal intent. Lana knew she had to keep calm otherwise she was finished.

She pulled the bow-string back as far as it would allow her. They were both distracted by a sudden burst of light that illuminated them. It lit up the night sky. The wolf fixed its gaze past her in the direction of the source of the light.

A deafening roar quickly followed it. A terrible noise which suggested great destruction. It sounded like thunder louder than she'd ever heard.

The wolf returned to its senses quicker than Lana. It took off at a sprint away from her. She let the arrow loose knowing it wouldn't reach its target – it didn't, flying several metres off her mark.

Cursing, she stood up and turned towards where the light and noise had come from. From where she was, it didn't take her long to figure out where. It was home.

She dropped her bow and quiver and took off, sprinting as fast as her legs would carry her.

~

Twigs and foliage whipped and clawed at her face as she flew through the forest, as though in a bid to slow her flight. She barely registered it, all thoughts were on home. Luckily her pursuit of the wolf hadn't taken her far. She was sure she'd first spotted it a lot further from home than where they'd ended up – the wolf having presumably led her back the way she'd come. It hadn't worried her at the time. She knew the forest well enough.

She didn't care. All thoughts of the beast she'd tracked, and the routes it had led her were now gone. She only cared about home. Were her mother and father okay? Had the noise definitely come from home? Lost in her reverie, she almost collided with a large root sticking out of the ground in front of her. On sheer instinct she managed to shift her weight and vault over it without slowing her pace.

After five or ten minutes – she wasn't sure – the trees began to thin out as she reached the edge of the clearing. She still couldn't see the cottage, but she could see a lot of smoke. A fire? But to what? Although that didn't explain the noise.

Her questions were soon answered as she caught a glimpse of the shattered, ruined remains of her home. The sight stopped her in her tracks. Standing around the carnage was a group of men.

There was maybe ten or twelve of them, standing in varying huddles of two's and threes. They wore strange dark armour she'd never seen before. Their breastplates had an image emblazoned on the front, but she couldn't make out what it was from the distance she was from them.

They weren't the King's soldiers, she knew that immediately. Their armour was silver, and they wore yellow cloaks. The armour these group of strangers wore seemed to play tricks with her eyesight, as though to try and avert her gaze away from it. She found the feeling made her a little uneasy. These men were different. Maybe from Helven, to the west? She didn't know. Her mind was a fog of questions with no answers.

It was at this point she noticed she'd been standing out in the open for far too long. Despite the gloom of the night, all it would take was for one of them to glance in her direction for little more than a couple of seconds and she'd be spotted for sure. She darted her head from side to side in search of cover. Being in the middle of a forest, it didn't take her long. A large oak stood a couple of feet away. She threw herself behind it, curling up against the rough bark.

She stayed where she was for a few seconds. Her breath came in sharp spasms. Her heart hammered in her chest and her legs felt wobbly and a little weak from her flight. She closed her eyes and steadied her breathing. She hadn't seen her mother or father in the short time she'd been staring at the men around her cottage. She could feel tears begin to form at the corner of her eyes. Later, she thought. She steeled her nerve and edged her way around the tree to see what was going on.

The men were talking and shouting. She couldn't hear what was being said, though they seemed to gravitate towards one man in the middle. He wore a large gauntlet on his right hand. He seemed to be their leader, pointing out orders to the others.

There was still no sign of her parents. Maybe they were out looking for her – she hoped.

She calculated what to do. She could run, but she couldn't leave without knowing where her parents were. Approaching was stupid as they'd just reduced her home to a smoking pile of rubble. Where were her parents?

As though reading her mind, two of the men dragged her mother's lifeless body from the wreckage. Her mother's hair lay matted over her face; her torn dress a collage of soot and blood. She stifled a sob which caught the attention of one of the men. She scrambled back round the oak and hoped to the Gods she hadn't been spotted.

She sat there as tears ran down her face. Her mother looked dead. Who were these men to do such a thing? Where was her father? He had to be under the rubble.

Staying low to the ground, she crawled around the oak for another look. The man who had glanced in her direction now had his back to her and was busy listening to orders from the leader. She sighed with relief.

They were looking in the opposite direction, as her father was pulled from the wreckage. He was struggling and shouting at them as he was dragged towards the leader. Using the distraction to her advantage, Lana crept closer to hear what was being said.

~

Argon looked down at the woman his men had unearthed from the carnage. Though the tangle of long dark hair covered the facial features beneath, he still recognised her. He'd known her once, long ago. He didn't feel bad she'd suffered at their hands. She was lucky, in fact. Her death had been quick. Instant. He appraised her prone figure the way a hunter would inspect a deer he'd just killed. The fact of the matter was that she was insignificant. Nothing.

The man on the other hand. His survival was a joy to behold. If he was being honest, he wasn't surprised. The man had always been impressive. It was just a shame he was on the wrong side of this fight.

He watched with mild amusement, as he thrashed and struggled to break free. The sight of the dead woman had reduced him to a blubbering wreck. It was really quite pathetic.

He stopped struggling the minute his eyes clapped on Argon. Recognition slowly dawned on his face. Argon relished every second of it, drinking it in like a fine wine.

"You," he shouted, pointing a finger at him.

Argon smiled, and nodded. "Yes. Me," he said, approaching him. He unsheathed his sword and drove the pommel into the side of his face. The man buckled, his legs going from under him. His men took the weight, keeping him upright. Argon nodded and the men let him drop to the ground.

He bent down and grabbed a handful of hair. He pulled the man closer so their faces were only inches apart. "I see my reputation proceeds me, Knight. Did you think I would not return? I told you all what was coming, but would you listen to reason?"

He drew back his fist and swung with all the strength he could muster, driving it into the Knight's jaw. His head snapped back from the blow. A mixture of blood, spittle, and teeth flew from his mouth.

"Your friend listened. He chose to fight and look where that got him. Dead. All because you and the High Lords wouldn't listen." He sheathed his sword.

"Your impatience will be your undoing, Argon," the Knight said, spitting out more blood. "We believed you. We just didn't believe you were the one to lead the fight." The Knight nodded at his men. "It looked like we were right. At what point did you turn?"

Argon had to stop himself from stabbing the knight there and then. It felt like he was standing before the High Lords all those years ago. He closed his eyes and shook his head. Letting the strong emotions pass through him. "What the Order thinks is of no consequence anymore." He knelt back down in front of the Knight. "They're all gone. The Knights of the Hour are vanquished. Put to the sword."

The Knight narrowed his eyes at Argon. "You lie," he said through gritted teeth. "The Hour have stood for a thousand years."

"Why would I lie? Besides, I was there. There's nothing left but ruin and bodies. I'd say see for yourself, but we both know that's not an option now is it?" he said, turning his gaze to the woman.

The Knight followed his glance, then scrambled over to his dead wife. His men were about to intervene. He waved them off.

Argon and his men watched in detached silence as the knight cradled his wife in a pathetic show of affection. His grief and pain came off him like heat. The Knight took a deep breath and pointed at Argon once more. "As long as there's one of us, our light shall be your undoing."

Argon laughed. The Knight's delusion of The Order was almost admirable. Almost. "Is that so?" he said.

He smiled, pulled a knife from his belt, and threw it at the Knight.

~

Lana crouched, hidden by a large boulder, in stunned silence. She couldn't believe her ears. Her father, a knight? Not once had she heard him or mother mention this. One of those reclusive knights who resided at the creepy temple near the border? He was a huntsman, not a knight.

Though it made her tuition, growing up, make a lot more sense. Especially the self-defence. Hours of hand to hand combat, and weapons training. She had asked him a couple of times why she needed the training. He'd told her the world was a hard place and a woman needed to be able to look after herself and not rely on a man for her own protection. At the time it seemed reason enough.

She cried silently as she watched her father cradle her dead mother. Her every pore ached for her to run over to them. Her heart broke as the sounds of his grief filled the night sky. She could feel a burning anger building within her soul towards the men who had caused it.

Their conversation had been brief. Most of it she didn't understand. What was coming? Who was her father's friend who had fought and died?

She'd almost cried out when the man in the black armour had thrown the dagger at her father. He'd fallen back, her mother rolling off his lap as the dagger had struck true. Time stopped. Was he dead?

Then, he got up. The dagger was sticking out of his chest, up to the hilt. Her panicked mind was still struggling with what to do. She was helpless. A spectator in events beyond her control. If she charged out to help her father, she would be peppered with arrows before she made a few steps. All she could do was watch.

~

Argon smiled as the Knight got to his feet – regardless of the nine inches of steel embedded in his chest. He really was a remarkable specimen. He unsheathed his sword and turned to Fargus, who'd been watching the exchange with interest. "Give him your sword," he ordered.

Fargus' eyes widened at the command. He looked like he was about to protest then thought better of it. It was the first time he'd seen Fargus pause at an order. He acquiesced, unsheathing his blade. He threw it at the Knight. It stuck in the ground a few inches from the Knight's feet. Argon smiled.

The Knight gripped the handle and pulled it from the ground, he tensed as the movement clearly caused him some discomfort. The Knight looked down at the dagger sticking out of his chest with what looked to Argon like mild irritation. He was going to enjoy this.

In one quick jerk, he pulled the knife out and threw it aside. Argon had expected him to throw it back in his direction. It was what he would have done. But where was the honour in such a move? Something unbefitting a Knight of the Hour. Argon had always felt 'honour' set you at a disadvantage.

Blood began to flow down the Knight's shirt. He pressed a hand over it. His hand glowed for a moment, sealing the deep gash. The Knight was weak. It wouldn't seal the wound for long.

"You're weak, Knight. The damage inside is beyond your skill. There are no Clerics left to heal the damage done."

The Knight's jaw set. "Let's get this over with."

They began to circle each other. Argon twirled his blade in smooth expert motions, moving the weapon as though it was an extension of his arm. The Knight narrowed his eyes, waiting for him to make the first move. A considerable amount of blood had run down the Knight's shirt already. How he was still standing – let alone carrying a sword and moving – was anyone's guess.

Argon feinted forward as though to make a lunge. He smiled as the Knight fell for the feint. He swung forward to counter a strike that had not come, realising only too late he had been duped. Argon sidestepped the attack and replied with two swipes, cutting into the Knight's back. He made sure they weren't deep. He wanted this to last as long as possible.

The Knight grunted as he stumbled forward, but remained standing. Argon couldn't help but be impressed by the Knight's endurance. He had been practically blown up in his house, and stabbed not long after. He'd seen cuts like that, on their own, drop men and women he'd fought countless times before.

However, the Knight wasn't completely unaffected. He'd lost a lot of blood. The wound on his chest was still open; his limited healing abilities failing to fully close it. A steady stream of blood was beginning to flow back down his chest. Droplets of blood were beginning to litter the forest floor. He was also panting hard from the exertion of their duel and his heart would be struggling for blood and oxygen.

It was time to end it.

Argon swung his sword in intricate arcs as he slowly approached for the killing blow. He feigned a swing to the right, then a swipe to the left. The Knight just managed to swat the blows aside, though he still suffered minor cuts.

The Knight attempted a clumsy stab. His desperation making him reckless. Argon spun around the move manoeuvring his sword aiming it towards the Knight's neck.

Then the unthinkable happened.

The blade passed through thin air. The Knight, in spite of his weakened state, managed to bend over backwards with lightning speed – the move must have caused him an excruciating amount of pain – avoiding the slice. Argon was now left wide open.

The Knight closed the gap between them and dropped his sword. Before Argon could react, his remaining knife was pulled from its sheath and driven into his eye.

White hot pain erupted through his skull as the blade reduced the soft tissue to pulp. He thought his throat was going burn as his scream filled the clearing. He could feel the coldness of the blade, buried deep in his eye socket. A warmness had begun to run down his cheek and neck.

He staggered back, the blade sliding out with a wet slop as a fresh stream of blood and tissue ran down his face. Despite the agony he was in, he still had enough of his wits to hold a hand over his eye and release some of his power. He felt his flesh burn as the wound closed. The acrid tang of scorched flesh crawled up his nose, almost making him vomit.

The Knight dropped to his knees, what remained of his strength leaving him. He paid no heed to Argon as he stamped his feet in misery. His attention was focused on something past him, towards the edge of the clearing. A sad smile was etched upon his face.

"My darling girl. You are now our last hope. You make me and your mother very proud. Do not worry, we shall see each other again in the halls of our fathers." He took a pained breath. "Now run, child. Hide from these men, lost to this world. Help will find you if you have faith. Now go."

In his state of perpetual agony, Argon was at a loss to what the Knight was rambling on about.

"There's a girl over there," he heard Fargus shout. "After her."

The smile was still plastered on the Knight's face as he dipped his head, and rested his chin onto his chest, as though at peace. It remained there, even after Argon had cut his head off his shoulders with one furious blow.

~

Lana's scream rivalled that of the man in the black armour. Hope had initially pulled at her when her father had drove the man in black armour's knife into his eye. It was soon dashed as she came to the realisation her father knew there was no way out for him.

She listened to the last words he would ever say to her, her heart shattering. Had he known she'd been hiding there the whole time?

She watched in horror as her father's head dropped to the ground. The image burned itself into her mind, never to leave it. She felt sick as she watched the blood spurt out of his open neck like a geyser, spattering the grounds that was her home. Her mind felt as though it was underwater. As though events were slow, moving in another time.

She soon came to her senses at the image of men running towards her, murderous intent on their faces. A couple of them stopped and took aim with their bows, a couple more threw what looked like round oversized rocks – though the last time she checked, rocks didn't glow. She turned and ran through the clearings edge and into the forest as fast as her legs would go.

Flashes of blue and white light lit up the woods around her, followed by an intense heat. She came to the conclusion those rocks were missiles of some kind. One exploded a few feet in front of her, sending thick splinters of bark and wood towards her; one of which struck her, embedding itself into her shoulder. She yelped in pain, but didn't let the injury slow her down. That would mean capture. That would mean death.

She vaulted over roots, and shrubs. Over rocks, and around ancient boulders. All the while arrows whipped past her head, and those strange missiles exploded everywhere she looked. One volley came so close as to burn her arm. The pain was intense. Ten times worse than a normal burn. She cried out but kept going.

She changed direction several times in attempt to shake them off, to lose them, but it was no use. She couldn't increase the gap. She could feel her legs burning in protest. She didn't know how long she would last.

The pain was almost too much to bear – physically and mentally. The adrenaline coursing through her veins was the only thing keeping her from the clutches of her assailants. She could hear them, close behind her. Cries of anger, and pure unadulterated hatred.

She was busy taking too many glances behind her when she almost ran off the edge of a narrow cliff overlooking the river. She skidded to a halt and turned around. The men would burst through at any moment. The fear she felt was almost debilitating.

Her head darted from right to left in a desperate attempt to find a route to take. To her dismay, she found there was nowhere to go. She was hemmed into a natural bottleneck in the terrain with only one way of escape. The way she'd came. The way her assailants were coming from.

The men in black armour suddenly pushed through and stood almost within touching distance. One soldier reached out to take her arm, a wicked gleam in his eye.

"There's nowhere to run, girl."

She took a step back, feeling the edge of the cliff with the heel of her boot.

"Now don't do anything stupid," another said, smiling.

She took a quick glance over her shoulder to the river below. It was so high. Tears ran down her face. This was it. This was how she was going to die. At the hands of men she didn't know, who didn't know her. Their reasons for killing her and her family she couldn't begin to guess.

In her dire situation she felt a desperate courage began to take root in her. Don't give them the satisfaction, she thought, as they began to creep closer to her, arms outstretched like claws.

She could feel heat rise in her chest and flow down her arms. In her frenzied hysteria, she hadn't noticed the change of expression on the men's faces; from leering hatred, to fear and confusion. She hadn't noticed the cliff edge had grown brighter. Or that the grass at her feet had begun to burn.

But then there was nothing to notice at all, as everything went white. Was this what dying felt like? She wasn't sure, and in that moment, she didn't care. She thought she heard a loud bang, but it could have been her imagination?

Then she was flying backwards. The men in black armour growing smaller, further away, above her. The cold of the river took her and the light turned to black.

Chapter Three - The Riverbank

Gren landed hard on his back with an audible thud, knocking the air from his lungs. Gasping in great heaves, each breath burning more than the last, he remained where he was, cursing himself for striking his line too soon.

His boat rocked from side to side – caused by the impact of his fall – the sky tilting from left to right in front of his sparkled eyesight. It was overcast, the dull grey of the clouds covering most of the blue, the threat of rain constant.

He rolled onto his front – as soon as the pain in his back had settled to a dull throb – and gingerly raised himself back to his feet, almost slipping overboard in the process.

He glanced down at the tangled mess his fishing line had become with a deep sense of foreboding. He knelt down and examined it; it spun and weaved in and out of itself in countless tangles. He sighed audibly. That'll be at least twenty minutes of unravelling, if it wasn't worse than it looked, he thought grimly.

The basket where he kept the fish he caught lay beside him. He looked sourly at its meagre contents: one fish, and that had taken more time than was necessary to land. Dread filled his guts like a lead weight. He would be the butt of every joke when he returned to the harbour and presented his glorious catch to the rest of the fishermen. It was a standing tradition to gently mock – as they put it – the fisherman who came back with the least amount of fish.

He wouldn't have a problem with their 'tradition' if he finished anywhere above last more often than not.

The fact he was the youngest and least experienced didn't seem to occur to them. He'd once made the mistake of voicing his concerns to his father one night after enduring a particularly heavy barrage of insults. He'd regretted the words the second they'd left his mouth. "It's their way of toughening you up, son," his father – the pacifist – had said. "To help you improve. To try harder, and get better."

The sage advice hardly helped his predicament. Their jokes and jibes didn't toughen him up. Neither did they help him get better. Suggestions on technique, and practical instruction would do that. The only thing it aided in was fuelling his self-doubt.

With a sigh he bent down and began the slow and monotonous process of untangling the mess lying in front of him. At first, one knot untangled would result in three more to replace it – the thin, wet line slipping away from him in resistance that almost seemed deliberate.

After half an hour everything was straightened out and ready to go back into the river. He wound his reel so only the lure and a couple of inches of line hung from the eyelet at the top of the rod. He swung the rod back, took aim, and whipped the rod forward.

Halfway through the cast, something wet and heavy struck the side of his head. He bit his tongue as his head whipped to the side, and he was sent sprawling back to the deck.

Confused and disorientated, he lay on his back holding the side of his face. His head felt like a troop of drummers were passing through it and the tip of his tongue throbbed. He could feel his eye already beginning to swell up. Amidst his groans, he heard a flapping noise coming from the other side of the boat.

He grabbed the side to pull himself up, accidentally flipping his rod overboard. Cursing, he looked towards the source of the noise. A large trout was writhing about on his deck. Had he been lucky enough to be in the right place at the right time? For a fish to leap out of the water and into his lap – or as it turned out, his face?

His questions were soon answered at the sound of laughter coming from behind him.

Finn and Tom were about twenty feet away cheering and waving at him from their boat looking pleased with themselves at – even he had to begrudgingly admit – making a decent shot of smacking him in the face with their fish.

His mood darkened. He suffered the most amount of jibes, gloating, and pranks from the two, testosterone addled, intelligence allergic idiots grinning at him from their boat. A boat which was bigger, more expensive, and in better condition than his own poorly assembled, ramshackle, pile of firewood.

"Thought you could use a hand with today's efforts, Gren. Tell me, will you be into double digits with the latest catch to land on your little shit-pile?" Finn shouted, presumably knowing the answer given Gren's track record.

"If it is, it's all he's bringing in today. He's lost his rod," Tom said, nudging Finn which elicited another bout of laughter.

Gren turned towards the edge of the boat where he had flipped the rod into the water. He peered into the river knowing full well it was lost to its murky depths. He began to scramble amongst his kit in an attempt to unearth a spare rod, which wasn't there. He only had the one.

"Maybe it's a sign, Gren," Finn said. "You're not cut out for fishing. Maybe you should just stick to farming like your peasant father."

Rage filled Gren. He hurried about his gear, and untied the oars. He had no idea what he would do when he reached them. It was two against one. Also, they were both twice his size and weight and had not long been accepted in the Lord's barracks to be trained as personal guard, up at the keep.

In his fury, he'd forgotten about the trout which had managed to wriggle and bounce its way towards him. He stood on it, slipped and stumbled backwards, tumbling over the edge into the river.

The ice-cold water seemed to envelope him like a shroud. It was dark and gloomy making it difficult to see which way was up, and which way was down. Although light, he could feel the gentle current pulling him.

A strange thought entered his mind – was he near his rod? He shook his head at the ridiculousness of it. A glint of sunlight caught his attention, breaking him from the absurd thought. He swam towards it.

He burst up, taking in deep lungful's of air. He turned, treading water, to see how far he was from the boat. It wasn't far. Maybe ten feet. If the current had been stronger, he could have surfaced anywhere. Lucky, he thought, not really believing it.

He managed to pull himself up and onto the boat on the second attempt, landing in a wet and miserable heap – the first only gave him a mouthful of water. He sat up and looked around to see if Finn and Tom were still nearby. He caught a glimpse of them disappearing around a bend in the river heading for home, having had enough fun for one afternoon at his expense.

He lay back down onto the deck, still breathing hard from the exertion. He felt like crying. Maybe Finn and Tom were right. Maybe he should just stick to farming.

He wrapped himself in a course blanket, picked up his oars, and made for home.

He'd travelled slowly along the river, letting the current take him back, more than his rowing, lost in his gloomy thoughts, when something on the riverbank caught his eye.

In no rush to reach the harbour to be subjected to some more ridicule – he'd had enough for one day – he pulled his oars in and stood up to get a better view. From his vantage point it looked like an oddly shaped piece of driftwood. Probably a large branch, he surmised, maybe broken off a tree further upstream.

He was about to sit down and continue his journey home, when he thought he could see an arm sticking out from under it. He narrowed his eyes. Was it just his imagination? He'd been up since the crack of dawn. It was probably his tired mind playing up. He took another look and sure enough, it was what looked like an arm.

Forgetting about his swollen eye, his aching head, or the fact he was soaked through, he jumped down and began the slow process of turning the boat – it was an effort against the current which was beginning to get stronger.

Once he reached the shore, he vaulted over the side landing with a splash – though it mattered not, he was already wet. He dragged the boat up the pebbled embankment, grimacing at the noise it made.

He ran up the steep embankment, the pebbles turning to mud which his boots sank into with every step. He reached the driftwood and sure enough, under it lay the body of a young woman.

He looked back towards his boat and the river behind it. As much as the day had been rotten, he still wanted to be near it.

He cast the absurd thought aside, given the situation he was in. He bent down next to the woman, his knees popping audibly, and with some effort managed to lift the branch off of her throwing it down the muddy slope.

To Gren she looked very much dead. She was deathly pale, and very wet. Her dark hair was plastered over her gaunt face. He looked at her shoulder were there seemed to be a piece of bark sticking out of it. Her clothes were burnt in sections which confused him given she'd been washed up from a river. Maybe her boat had caught fire, he guessed.

He shook his head at the sight. "I'm sorry," he said, not knowing why he said it.

He now had a dilemma to deal with. What was he going to do? A number of options sprang to mind: the first was leaving the body and fetching the harbour master. But that was not good. He wasn't confident he'd be able to find the spot: He could leave the body and pretend he hadn't seen it. No, that wasn't right. This was someone's daughter.

That left the only other choice he could think of. The right one. He'd carry her back to his boat and take her in.

A howl in the distance startled him. He looked up at the sky, a deep red had settled behind the grey of the clouds. It would be dark soon. Wolves had been spotted around this area of the forest of late, unusual as they tended to stay higher up towards the mountains.

He shivered, suddenly feeling vulnerable. What if there was one watching him right now? It was not a comforting thought.

The image of him being ripped apart by a hungry pack of wolves sprung him into action. Pushing aside the fact he was about to touch a dead body, Gren gently rolled her onto her back. Her arms flopped to the side, splashing a little in the mud.

Suddenly, a gush of river water erupted from the woman's mouth like a geyser. Gren just about fled to his boat, leaving his skin behind with the not so dead woman.

He sat there, dumbstruck, as she turned herself onto all fours and proceeded to hack and cough up the rest of what she'd swallowed. Oddly, as he watched her retching, he found he was amazed at how much fluid a human body could intake.

He snapped himself out of the daydream he'd climbed into and rushed over to her aid, kicking up mud and water as he struggled to gain purchase on the soft ground.

He knelt down beside her and began to gently pat her back – this was also the right thing to do in the current circumstance, he told himself.

"You're okay," he said. "Get it all up. You know for a second I thought you were de..." Her head snapped round as the realisation of not being alone must have dawned on her.

Her eyes darted around in all directions giving her an almost feral look. Then they locked onto his. For a brief moment they remained where they were, unable to break eye contact. It was in this moment Gren thought she had the most beautiful eyes he had ever seen. Though bloodshot and wild, he found they contained a deep intelligence and awareness. They were a pale blue, like the sky above the mountains on a clear winter's day. It felt like she was looking into his soul.

He couldn't look away.

Their gaze was broken as she lunged at him with incredible speed. They rolled down the embankment in a tangle of arms and legs sending sprays of mud and water into the air. They stopped just short of the river's edge, his head slamming back against the pebbles – not hard enough given today's exploits, he thought ruefully.

He was in the middle of spluttering out an 'I don't mean you any harm' when the cold steel of a knife pressed against his throat. Where the knife had come from, he had no idea. He hadn't noticed one when he'd first approached her unconscious self.

"Who are you? Where am I? Where are

the bastards who killed them? What happened to me? There was a light..." She trailed off, reaching up with her knife hand to press her fist against her forehead.

Gren raised his head, she looked down at him as if trying to regain her train of thought. She lowered the knife back down against his throat. He lowered his head back down onto the riverbank.

If he wasn't so scared out of his wits, he would have been able to answer the first two questions – the rest he had no idea. Instead he merely tried to gesture his answer with waving hands and some more spluttering.

Smooth with the ladies as always Gren, he thought. Even with the half drowned, half starved, all crazy ones. It was in these rare moments he had no doubts about why the world seemed to want to punish him.

The steel pressed against his throat a little harder. Her eyes bored into his suggesting his last answer wasn't good enough. It was amazing what a little of your own blood running out of you could do to bring you back to your senses.

"I'm Gren. I live on the outskirts of the city of Dalton's Hill, three miles downriver. I didn't know anyone had been killed," he blurted out, hoping to the Gods it had been coherent.

He watched, helpless, as this strange woman he didn't know was musing whether to open him up where he lay based on the babbling answer he'd just given her. It didn't fill him with hope.

Instead of spilling his life's blood onto the cold wet mud, she dropped the knife. Her eyes rolled back into her head, then collapsed on top of him, unconscious.

As they both lay there, the river flowing gently behind them, Gren cried out in relief.

Chapter Four - Return of an Exile

A mist had descended upon the river like a blanket, between the thick forest that flanked it. The current was calm, the water gentle as it flowed. Emerging from the fog on a small, thin craft, stood the hooded man; one hand stretched out at his back guiding the small boat. His hand glowed slightly from the use of his power which guided the small vessel to his will.

He knew he drew close to where he was travelling to; his strong eyesight could see the small trail of smoke over the trees at the top of the incline. He flicked his fingers sending the boat towards the river's edge. It obeyed, sending the craft cutting through the water into a wide arc finally stopping where it met the land.

He took a few steps to the end and hopped off gracefully. He turned and dragged it up the bank so as it wouldn't be swept downstream should the current grow stronger in his absence. Happy where the boat was, he ventured into the forest.

He took his time ascending the incline in the land so as not to slip and fall back down. He could feel the undergrowth was damp so he took each step with care. Taking in his surroundings, with its smells and vast array of animal and plant-life, he hadn't realised how much he'd missed the Great Forest. It's rich array of aromas and beautiful scenery usually brought him peace.

But not today. Or any day in the near future, he thought grimly. He stopped a moment to find his bearings. He looked ahead into the gloom. His destination wasn't far. He took a breath and marched on.

Within the hour he had reached the clearing his old friends resided at. A clearing in the woods only he and a few others knew of. Though, he was the only one alive now that knew.

Images of death and destruction at the temple still plagued his thoughts. Images that would haunt him for the rest of his days. He shivered, shaking the sorrow he felt building within him to the back of his mind.

He pushed past some low hanging branches and caught sight of his worst fears made flesh. The cottage was in complete ruin. There was nothing left. Grief swept over him like a wave crashing against rocks on the shore. His breath caught in his throat.

He'd suspected the worst the second he'd seen the smoke from the river, but didn't want to believe it at the time. Strangely, most of the smoke wasn't coming from the burnt remains of the cottage, but a small camp fire beside it.

Two men wearing black armour were huddled around it; their hand's outstretched as if the act pulled more heat from the flames. From the look of the scene in front of him, he surmised these men, at the very least, were responsible for the condition of the cottage. Anger swept over him like a veil.

He broke from cover, not caring about the noise he made. Startled, the two men glanced in his direction then quickly rose, picking up their weapons.

"Stop," one of the men said, holding up his bow, aiming for the hooded man's heart. "What business do you have here?"

The hooded man didn't answer, but continued to walk towards them, letting his fury and rage build within him, giving him focus. His hand slowly reached under his cloak, finding the hilt of his sword underneath. He coiled his fingers around the grip, feeling the leather creak beneath his grasp.

"I said stop, vagrant. Remove your hood, and take your hand out from under the robe... slowly." He turned to his comrade, but didn't take his eyes from his target. "I like to see the face of the man I kill."

The other man smirked, drawing his sword; the blade scraping as it slide from its scabbard. "I'm not fussy either way. Vagrant or not, dead is dead."

He began to step away from his partner – presumably to skirt around to his back. At the moment, the hooded man wasn't interested with him. Just the man aiming an arrow to his heart.

He was twenty yards away from the bowman, the gap closing fast with each step.

The bowman let the arrow loose. It struck the ground two feet away. He quickly pulled another from his quiver. Still the hooded man proceeded.

"This is your last chance. The next one puts you down. I promise you that."

"Try it," the hooded man replied, coldly.

The bowman didn't hesitate as he let go of the arrow. It flew from the bow at lightning speed, but the hooded man was quicker. In a blur he unsheathed his sword; its flawless surface catching the moonlight. He turned and whipped it down, cutting the arrow in two as it passed, reducing it to splinters.

The bowman could only gape as the hooded man closed the gap and swung the blade with expert precision cutting his head off in a spray of blood and gore. The head toppled over the bowman's shoulder; the look of astonishment still etched upon its features. His body remained standing where it was for a few seconds before it dropped to the ground like a bag of spuds.

The other man was quicker than his dead friend to regain his composure. He lunged at the hooded man from behind, hoping to skewer him whilst his attention was focused elsewhere. The hooded man smirked grimly as he spun around the attack, using the momentum to add force to his swing. The sword cut into the man's neck at a downward angle. It sheared bone and tissue as if it were made of butter, finally resting at his stomach. He slid it out and watched in detached silence as the man dropped to the ground, his life's blood spilling out onto the forest floor.

He bent down and tore off a piece of the man's surcoat. He wiped his blade clean with it then threw it aside. He sheathed his sword and approached the pile of rubble at the centre of the clearing. Towards its middle, small rivulets of smoke were still seeping their way out of the gaps, disappearing up into the night's sky.

He bent down and picked up a small piece of masonry from the bottom of the ruined cottage. He brought it up to his nose and inhaled. His face twitched slightly at the sour aroma it gave off; part recognition, part nauseated. He threw the rock back onto the pile. Fire-sand. Made by the mountain tribes, though he knew the Watalla were not responsible for this.

He rose, sighing audibly. His legs were tired. He'd spent the last few weeks travelling hard, and fast. He looked to the wreckage, his throat tightening.

Not fast enough.

He shook his head and cleared his throat. This was just the beginning of what was to come. The war had begun and the sad thing was, no one knew it.

He slowly walked around the pile of rocks until he came across two bodies. The two bodies of friends from long ago. He approached them reverently; his hands clasped behind his back, his head bowed.

"Oh, my friends," he whispered. "I thought being hidden here would spare you from harm and bloodshed. I'm so very sorry." A tear escaped his eye and tumbled down his cheek. He made no move to wipe it.

They should have had peace, he thought sadly. "I will bury you with full rights and honours, my friends. It's the least you deserve."

His gaze fell once more upon the ruined pile that was their home. Concern etched his face. He hadn't been to this clearing in nearly twenty years, but he knew a third resident lived here.

He removed his robes and unbuckled his sword belt, laying them next to his friends. He climbed to the top of the pile and began to slowly dismantle it piece by piece.

After an hour he stood back, panting from the labour. Sweat ran down his face, giving it a glossy sheen. As he'd reached the bottom of the pile, he'd grown more relieved with each piece of stone he'd removed, as he found nothing sinister within.

He turned to his dead friends. "I'll find her. If she's alive, I'll find her. I promise, on my honour. I will guide and protect her as we discussed so very long ago." He glanced over at the dead soldiers. "If this day would come."

He strode over to his belongings and put them back on. His sword resting against his leg once more gave him a sense of completeness. He never left it from his person for very long.

He began to assess the area. Working out how his friends had perished at the hands of their assailants. It was at this point he'd wished he'd kept one of the men alive – his anger had got the better of him, he thought ruefully, though he didn't regret it.

There had been more than two of them. The exact number he wasn't certain of. It could have been six. It could have been sixteen. They'd approached the cottage from all sides. They'd then lain their explosives at each corner, stepped back, and set it alight destroying the cottage.

He gazed down at the woman. From the look of her, she'd died in the blast – a blessing it had been a quick death. He bent down and patted her hand gently, mouthing a silent prayer.

He raised himself and paced over to the front of the cottage – what used to be, anyway. His other friend had been dragged from the wreckage. He followed two drag marks in the ground, flanked by two sets of footprints.

He knelt down and touched the marks where they stopped. Then he was beaten. He swivelled round on his hips and followed a series of steps and swipes in the ground, veering to and fro in various directions, but enough to suggest they belonged to two people.

There had been a fight – a fairer fight

than to begin with. His friend must have either been given a sword, or had been lucky enough to find one nearby. The evidence around him suggested it was the former.

He stood up and, following the patterns of the fight on the ground, began to play out the fight in his mind. His friend had fought valiantly, as he expected he would. Dried blood still remained, growing thicker as he followed the pattern the closer he got to his friend's body. He'd been wounded heavily before the final blow.

He noticed there was a separate pool of dried blood across from his friend's body which told him he'd injured the man who'd eventually killed him. He squatted down, taking a closer look. Quite badly he suspected. He smiled for his friend. Good, he thought.

He rose back to his feet. He would find the rest of those responsible.

He reached up and ran his hand through his hair. That accounted for the couple. It didn't tell him what had happened to the girl. Where was she? Had she still been living with her parents? Had she got married and moved away? Had she died in the years he had been gone from these lands? He didn't know.

Frustration plagued him. Exasperated, he took a seat on a nearby log, and rested his face into his hands. He suddenly felt tired and weary.

After a moment of quiet meditation, he

lifted his head up, staring into the woods. Before he settled his head into his hands once more, one boulder in particular caught his attention. A large chunk was missing in the middle of it. On its own that wasn't unusual. Rocks came in all shapes and sizes. It was just the hole in this rock didn't look natural.

It looked as though something had blasted a hole through it.

Recently.

He looked back at the cottage, then back at the boulder. He nodded to himself, smiling. He walked over to the boulder and ran a scarred hand over its rough surface. The hole was ringed with black soot that came away to the touch. He brought his hand up to his nose. Fire-sand.

It was a fairly large hole; no bigger than a man's head. She must have been hiding behind it. He followed its path towards the forest. The trees and rocks beyond were damaged in varying degrees. She must have been discovered, then pursued.

The realisation dawned on him. The poor child must have witnessed her parents murder. His heart wrenched at the thought, turning quickly to fury. And if she's alive, she's all alone in the world, he thought sadly.

The hooded man followed the path of destruction through the forest, away from the clearing. After ten minutes of tracking the trail, he reached a small cliff edge overlooking the river. She had been cornered to this point. Then what?

He looked down towards the rapids. It was twenty, maybe thirty feet. He looked down at his feet. He noticed the ground was charred in places. This wasn't making any sense, but he was intrigued all the same.

He tried to picture the scene in his mind. She'd ran to the edge and turned around only to be faced with her assailants. He tried to put himself in her shoes. If he was outnumbered, unarmed, and cornered, there was only one possible way of escape. He looked down to the river.

She'd jumped – or was pushed.

It still didn't explain why the ground was burnt in places. The girl and her parents' killers were at close quarters, so the explosives would have been out of the question. And there was no evidence to suggest she'd been killed; there was no sign of blood like there was back at the clearing.

He took another glance towards the river, resolve beginning to kindle in his heart.

If she'd jumped into the river and somehow survived...

The river ran towards Oakhaven. From here it wasn't that far. It wasn't that impossible.

Hoping he was right, and making the right decision, he ran back through the trees, disappearing into the forest.

Chapter Five – Diplomacy

In Oakhaven, the royal court was abuzz with activity. Lords of the King's interior council had been called for an emergency session. Carriages were queued on the road leading to the council chambers. The great bells within the huge towers had been ringing all morning, their tolls carrying for miles around.

Noblemen adorned in fine clothes their wealth provided, ascended the stone steps in great huddles. Silently looking down on them were the statues of long dead kings flanked on either side, leading up to the iron-oak doors; standing fifteen feet in height.

Rumours and gossip were thrown back and forth, some more outlandish than others. Regardless of what version, they all sang the same tune.

The temple of the Knights of the Hour had been destroyed, its resident's put to the sword.

Once the lords were settled inside the great hall, the bells ceased, only to be replaced with the sounding of the royal horns silencing the room. The King had arrived.

King Hal entered. At six and a half feet, his huge frame took up the majority of the space between the door-frames. His thick black beard rested on his chest, his eyes serious and alert as he made his way into the council chambers. Queen Isabel hung onto his arm gracefully. Her small stature a stark contrast to her husbands. Her golden hair was plaited, decorated with ribbons of gold and white, spilling over one shoulder and down to her waist. Like the King, her head was held high as they made their way to the front of the room. The lords bowed as they passed.

They climbed the stone steps to the royal podium. The Queen unhooked her arm from the King's and took a seat to the side. King Hal waited until she was settled, then strode over to the stand which held his sceptre. He picked it up and carried it to the centre of the podium, were he slammed the butt of it onto the marble floor, the sound reverberating around the room silencing the chatter.

The guards at the entrance closed the oak doors. The meeting had begun.

A servant took the sceptre from the King, who turned and addressed his noblemen. "News from the west?" the King boomed. He began to pace, his hands clasped behind his back. "Are the rumours true? Or have I been listening to gossip like some washerwoman?"

Skallen, Commander of the royal army, and brother to the King, stepped forward. He was smaller than his brother, though no man could claim he was short in stature. His hair was cut short, and his beard was neatly cropped into a point. He nodded, his eyes sharp. "Your Grace, the rumours are indeed true. The temple is in ruin. Intelligence has informed me the Knights were betrayed from within." He paused a moment, taking a breath. "Reports seem to suggest they were infiltrated by agents serving Helven."

The hall filled with noise as the lords began to shout their outrage. Skallen didn't turn around, he merely stared at his brother, his gaze cold. The King pursed his lips, his eyebrows furrowing.

King Hal let the lords vent their anger for a moment as he digested the information. He pulled at his beard with a huge hand, letting the course hair pass through his grasp. After a time, he clapped his hands together. "Silence," he roared.

The cacophony ceased once more. The King looked down at his brother – the crease still etched upon his brow. "Is there any evidence to support these reports, Commander?"

Skallen waved a hand towards the back of the room were a military aid made his way to the front carrying a bundle of cloth. The lords parted as the young lad made his way to the front, looking very much like a mouse amongst lions. He looked to his superior who nodded for him to proceed. The aid unrolled the cloth. It was partially burned with spatters of what appeared to be dried blood. It didn't hide the fact it was a banner. A banner bearing the image of a sword against the backdrop of the rising sun.

The sigil of the Knights of the Hour.

The hall filled with worried murmurs, and hushed comments that didn't seem to be aimed at anyone in particular. The King glanced up at the balconies which surrounded the hall. It was as if something had caught his eye. He looked back down, studying the damaged banner, trying to decipher the meaning of it. He shook his head, a look of great sadness marring his features.

His eyes locked back to the Commander's. Skallen hadn't so much as glanced at the banner lying at his feet. His features remained stoic, unreadable. "Did your men find anything else besides death and ruin?"

"No, your Grace."

The King nodded solemnly to himself, his eyes flitting to the balcony once more before he paced the podium again. "Tell me, Commander, My Lords, why would Helven risk such a move? All-out war, when our two Kingdom's have enjoyed a steady peace for centuries?"

"My men are investigating as we speak, your Grace. They will report their findings within the month," Skallen said. He turned to the Lords. "However, in my opinion, it hardly stretches the imagination as to why our neighbours would break the treaty. My scouts will find evidence which will condemn Helven soon enough. As you are all aware, Helven have long envied our land's rich source of iron oak, which is scarce within their rocky borders.

I would say the reason is staring us in the face. They've managed, somehow, to destroy the Knights of the Hour leaving the playing field open to do as they please. There's no-one else with the manpower to destroy the Hour. In their own home no less."

"So you say, Commander," King Hal said, adding extra emphasis on the title. "What would you have your king do?"

Skallen didn't appear to notice the King's tone. He began to pace in front of the assembly himself. "I would raise the banners. Send our armies towards the border, through the mountain pass. It's only a matter of time before they send a force past the mountains and through the great forest towards our towns and cities," he said, gesturing wildly. "The less time we give them the better."

Many of the lords voiced their approval. The King took in the scene, knowing his options were growing more limited. "Perhaps we should send an envoy to King Richard, to make sense of this madness."

Skallen nodded at the King's suggestion a second before shaking his head. As though an argument was discussed, then settled in his head. "An excellent suggestion, my King, though I would think it a fruitless gesture. If we send a representative of the court over the border, we would be left waiting on a reply which might not come.

Giving them as much time as they needed to muster their men and cross the border. We cannot take that chance." He paused. "But, we shall do as you command, your Grace."

"Very well. There seems to be little choice. Organise the army then, Commander. We shall see where this takes us. To war if need be."

Skallen bowed to his brother. "Your will, my King."

The King nodded. "As of this other problem. The temple. You say your scouts have investigated the temple and its grounds, but have they searched the surrounding areas? The mountain tribes? I believe the Knights were friendly with those stubborn fools residing up there. Would it be prudent to order the scouts to widen their search?"

Skallen raised an eyebrow at the suggestion. "The tribes? It is possible, but given our current predicament I'd think it a waste of our resources. There's nothing there but destruction. I believe there are no Knight's left."

The King narrowed his eyes at his brother. "Is that so?" The King looked up towards the balcony. "I think Lord Kerr would disagree with you."

~

Emerging from the shadows, Lord Kerr, Knight of the Hour, watched as Skallen's face changed from surprise to outrage. Kerr's fists were clenched so hard the nails had begun to break the skin on his palms, which were damp – and not due to the heat in the stuffy council chambers.

"A Knight in our capital," Skallen shouted. "Why was I not informed? I am Commander of the Army."

A dark shadow passed over King Hal's features at his brother's tone. "You were not told because it is at my pleasure whether or not to inform you who resides within my city, Commander of the army or not," the King bellowed at his brother.

Skallen bowed. "Forgive me for speaking out of turn, your Grace. How long has he been in the city?"

Kerr could feel the anger coursing through him, it was almost overwhelming. Skallen spoke as though he wasn't there; like he'd just discovered a rat in his kitchen and wondered how it had got there in the first place. He felt he'd enjoy nothing more than to vault over the railing and smash the arrogant fool's teeth down his throat.

"For centuries, the capital has been home to at least one Knight of the Hour. It has been an agreement between the Hour and the crown since the old wars, long ago," King Hal said.

Kerr removed his hood; his hair fell in tangles down to his shoulders. He gripped the railing, looking down at the procession. He could feel the eyes of all the lords on him like ants crawling over his skin. The King looked up at him with sadness, but it was Queen Isabel who caught his eye. She looked at him with the deepest sorrow. She seemed to be the only one in the room that looked like she genuinely felt for his loss. If it was true.

"Don't worry, Skallen, I will be returning to the temple in due course," he said, enjoying the look on the Commander's face at being addressed without title.

"The temple, my Lord? You've heard what the Commander has told us. As much as you dislike my brother, it was my men who reported their findings," the King said, drawing their attention away from each other.

"With all due respect, I will see for myself, your Grace."

The King's expression turned dark for just a second. "And what of the threat of war between Grunald and Helven?" he boomed from his podium.

Kerr understood what was at stake between the two realms. He was concerned war would start out of rashness as each side worried what the other would do. There was every chance Helven knew nothing of events at the temple – if they were true. The King was right with the suggestion of an envoy. But his brother held too much sway with the King. The fool was eager for war.

"I am but one man, your Grace. I will travel back to my home. If your scouts' reports are true, there will be a lot of bodies to bury. To aid in their ascension to the halls of their fathers. If I am the last of my kin, the responsibility rests with me. I will also use the time to conduct my own investigations. Be assured," he said, turning his gaze directly to Skallen. "I will find answers and deal with those responsible if they are not to my taste."

He didn't think the King would accept his answer. He wasn't disappointed, as the giant monarch took a step forward and pointed a finger at him. "You will do no such thing," King Hal shouted. "As much as news from the temple is tragic, must I remind you of your sworn duty as a Knight of the Hour? Haven't you been listening to this council meeting? We are on the brink of war. You wish to waste time when it could be spent preventing it. As you were sworn to do."

Kerr couldn't believe his ears. Rage pulsed through his veins at the complete dismissal of his loss. "A waste of time?" he bellowed. "This matter could be settled with a simple envoy, like you suggested. But your idiot brother is so intent on war, and holds so much influence over your court, you're blind to reason."

King Hal, not used to being addressed in such a manner, went scarlet with rage. Kerr thought the King was a good man, but it didn't matter when his court was full of men like Skallen; snivelling courtiers with their own agendas.

Skallen beat the King to a reply. "How

dare you speak to your King in such a disrespectful tone."

"I am a Knight of the Hour. I have no King," he said, stunning the room to an eerie silence. It was technically true. The Knights of the Hour didn't pledge allegiance to either king, they merely acted as mediators, stepping in when either side threatened the other, disrupting the peace. Although he conceded this was probably not the time to remind the King of this. Kerr knew he'd been baited by Skallen, but he didn't care, he was so angry he couldn't stop the words spilling from his mouth.

Kerr didn't wait for a reply. He turned and made for the exit as the King's fury broke the silence in a barrage of incoherent cursing. Three guards suddenly emerged from the doorway, blocking his path – presumably signalled by Skallen the moment he'd been announced to the room.

"Stop in the name of the King," one of the guards ordered.

Kerr shook his head at them. "Get out of the way, lads. I don't want to hurt you."

"It's three against one, son," the guard said. "I don't care if you're some fancy Knight. You're coming with us to answer to the King."

Kerr sighed. "Very well."

Without warning Kerr sprinted forward with incredible speed, surprising the men. He drove his fist into the first guards face, breaking his nose. The soldier gave out a high-pitched whine as he slumped to the floor clutching his blood-spattered face.

He dropped to a crouch, spinning, as the next guard ran towards him, sword raised. He swept a leg out sending the guard up in the air. The soldier landed awkwardly on his neck with a sickening crack, his sword clattering to the stone floor. He continued onto the final guard, rising and bringing his forehead up which smashed against the guard's jaw sending him sprawling backwards.

Using the guard's temporary incapacitation, Kerr disappeared through the exit and down the stairwell suspecting this wasn't the last he'd hear of this.

~

Kerr had managed to evade the King's guard despite the commotion he'd caused – although it could have been avoided if King Hal had kept his brother in check. He was a good King, loved by his people, respected by his nobility. Kerr felt it was somewhat spoiled by that worm, Skallen, using his status as the King's brother to meddle in affairs above his station.

He'd felt guilty injuring the three men on the balcony – well, a little guilty. They were only carrying out orders, and a little eager to impress their sovereign. He would make amends when he returned.

If he returned, he thought grimly.

Keeping to the shadows, he slowly made his way down to the outer ring of the city, closest to the outer walls which surrounded the capital; twenty feet of thick stone enclosing the city against its gated harbour on the opposite side.

He couldn't take the most direct route to his lodgings; avoiding sentries whenever he spotted them, using the maze of side-streets and alleyways to skirt around them. He couldn't be sure how long it would take the palace authorities to dispense a warrant for his arrest throughout the city, but he felt it was best to err on the side of caution.

It was dark and it had begun to rain, giving the cobbled road a slick sheen, as he approached the tavern where he rented a room. A small stream of rainwater was already flowing down either side of the street taking the shit and accumulation of litter with it.

He'd arrived in the capital on secondment from his brethren, to keep him away from temple matters and out of trouble he no doubt suspected. He chose to rent a room as far away from the palace as possible. Only the King knew of there being an Hour's presence in the city, he thought it unwise to take the chance of discovery by men like Skallen if he resided closer.

He took a quick glance behind him before he entered the inn, making sure he hadn't picked up a tail. The street was empty. Satisfied, he pushed through the door out of the rain and into the warmth.

The smell of sweat and stale ale hit him immediately. The bar was full of patrons, with nearly every table filled with a mixture of market sellers, harbour workers, and a few unsavoury looking characters within the booths to the rear of the room.

Banks, the innkeeper, nodded to him as he passed. Kerr nodded back. He didn't like the man, but his ale was good, and the room he provided suited his needs. He was generally left alone which he liked.

He passed through the doorway at the end of the bar which led to the stairwell up to the rooms – almost succumbing to the urge of ordering a flagon of ale.

He got halfway up the stairs, when a hushed voice called up to him. He turned around to find Grace, one of Banks' barmaids looking up at him. "My Lord," she said. She didn't know he was a Knight of the Hour. Since they'd met, for some reason, she'd insisted on calling him 'Lord'.

She glanced around nervously, as though someone might overhear her. "Grace, I'm in a hurry," he said a little more tartly than he'd intended.

"I know, my Lord." She glanced around once more. He really didn't have time for games. "The innkeeper, my Lord. He'd kill me if he found out I told you."

Kerr leaned on the bannister. "Told me what, Grace?" He was starting to lose his patience.

She took a few steps up the stairs towards him. She nodded in the direction of his room. "There's men waiting for you in there, my Lord. Bad ones."

She had his attention now.

"How many, Grace? Are they armed?" he asked, glancing up the stairs.

"Four. They have cudgels. Probably have knives concealed under their cloaks too I'd wager. You best leave now."

Her concern for his well-being touched him. He looked into her eyes. She genuinely cared if something happened to him. He felt a little bad for being short with her. His features softened as he put a hand on her shoulder. "I'm not leaving without my belongings, Grace." He smiled. "I think now would be a good time to take your break."

She returned his smile with one of her own, which lit up her face. She really was comely, he thought. She darted forward and kissed him on the cheek, taking him unawares. Then she was gone, through the back door in a twirl of skirts.

He stood there for a moment, staring like an idiot at the empty doorway she'd disappeared through. He slowly raised a hand and touched his cheek. He could still feel the wetness her kiss had left behind. She had always been pleasant to him, giving him extra portions at mealtimes, making a beeline for him whenever she saw him come through the front door to the inn. He realised then he'd miss her when he left the capital. It was strange how you only missed certain things when they weren't there anymore, he thought.

He shook his head and rested his gaze to the top of the stairs. He had four guests to entertain.

Keeping his footsteps light, he stealthily crept up the stairs – keeping his footsteps to the edges of the wooden boards, lessening the chances of them creaking and alerting his erstwhile guests to his presence.

He reached his door and slowly lowered himself down onto his stomach, remaining to one side so as not to cast a shadow under the door. Grace had been right. Four pairs of feet stood in his room; two to the left of the door, one at the back of the room, and one to the right. He smiled in spite of the severity of his predicament.

A gnawing feeling was beginning to take root in the back of his mind. It didn't feel right. Not long after leaving the palace, four men – possibly from the thieves' guild – were waiting to ambush him in his room. Men who could not have known whether his presence at the royal court would have caused the scene it had, or whether his presence had gone unnoticed. Someone knew who he was, and where he slept.

And they wanted rid of him.

He stood staring at the door. His order was rumoured to be all but destroyed. The King and his court couldn't see past petty squabbles with their neighbours – only seeing the news of his tragic circumstances as an inconvenience instead of possibly being part of the same picture.

He suddenly felt alone in the world, and angry at being dismissed when he needed help most of all. His order had helped create the peace the two kingdoms enjoyed. Couldn't they, just this once, put aside their petty scheming and power-grabbing for one second and return the favour.

No, he thought sourly, he had four men hiding in his room, awaiting his return so they could, at the very least, beat him to a bloody pulp. That was all the thanks he was getting.

He let his rage consume him, giving him focus. He stepped in front of the door and drove his boot through it with all the strength he could muster. The lock burst, the door flying open violently. It struck the two men standing behind it with a crack, sending them crashing into the wall.

The other two remained where they were, staring at him in surprise, open mouthed and gawking.

He didn't give them a chance to regain their wits. He rushed over to the table and picked up a clay jug which was half full of ale. The cheeky bastards had been having a casual drink as they'd waited on him, he thought incredulously. He smashed it over the face of the man who had been standing at the back of the room, sending shards of jug, flesh, and blood onto the floorboards.

Unfortunately for him, he was too close to the open window. He staggered back, holding his ruined face, and tumbled out of it. His bemused cry was quickly replaced with a wet thump as he landed on the cobbled road below.

Kerr turned to the last man, who was staring in disbelief out the window to where his friend had disappeared through. Kerr rushed over to him in two strides and slammed his forehead into his face. His head whipped back, blood exploding from his nose and mouth, spraying over the ceiling. He fell onto the bed in a heap.

Kerr turned to the doorway he'd came through. The two men he'd hit with the door were blocking his path. They stood coiled, ready for a fight, armed with nasty looking cudgels held aloft. Kerr sighed, as he bent down and pulled his War-hammer from under the bed. He swung it up, resting it on his shoulder as though it weighed nothing. The fight, as well as the blood, seemed to drain from both their faces at the sight of Kerr's weapon.

"Now gentlemen, you've seen what I can do unarmed." He patted the head of the War-hammer. "Just think what I can do with this old girl. She's always game for making new friends," he said, a wicked grin spreading across his face.

The two men held up their hands, and slowly backed out of the room. They fled, pushing at each other in an attempt to beat the other to leave first. The sounds of their panicked flight disappeared to nothing as Kerr packed his belongings. From the window he could hear them pick up their comrade, and carry him up the street.

Kerr looked down at the unconscious man on his bed. He was sorely tempted to haul him out of the window, but decided against it. He glanced around the carnage that was his room. He'd done enough. He shook his head and left the man where he was.

When he entered the bar, everyone stared at him, though nobody made eye contact. Banks had a look of fear in his eyes which told Kerr he probably knew what the four men had intended and was likely the one who'd let them into the room.

He made for the front door, anyone in his path quickly moved out of it. Before he left, he turned back around to face Banks. He tapped a finger to his temple. "I have a long memory, Innkeeper." Banks gulped audibly as Kerr took to the street, and to his horse.

Chapter Six - Bacon, Eggs, and Fractured Memories

Lana walked through the woods, the sun casting a warm glow through the canopy above. She was in her bare feet, the grass comforting on the soles. She could feel the blades of grass between her toes, warm and enveloping. She felt safe.

She strolled across the clearing towards the quaint little cottage she called home. It looked picturesque in front of the rich green of the forest behind it. Smoke billowed slowly out of the chimney in thick plumes. Her mother must have started breakfast, she surmised. She picked up her pace at the prospect of a warm meal.

At the far side, in front of the barn, her father was busy chopping wood. He raised his head, noticing her approach, and waved a hand at her. Something was off about him, she thought. She just couldn't put her finger on it. She cast the thought aside and waved back.

She hopped up onto the porch, the wood creaking as it took her weight. The front door was open. She stepped through, heat and the aroma of bacon and eggs filling her nostrils. Her stomach growled. She was starving. She ran her hands along the walls as she headed down the hall towards the kitchen.

She was greeted by the sight of her mother busying herself over the stove. She had her back to her, humming a happy tune to herself. The sound of food sizzling in the pan made her mouth water. She said hello to her mother, who didn't reply, just continued humming. She approached her and touched her mother's arm. She stiffened.

It was ice cold.

Her mother went quiet and stopped what she was doing. She went rigid, dropping the utensils she'd been using. She turned around to face her daughter. Lana stifled a scream.

Her mother's face was chalk white, save for a bloody gash that ran along the length of her forehead, revealing her skull. She noticed her eyes were also white. There were no pupils either, or any colour at all in fact. Just white – like pebbles that had been bleached by the sun.

Her mother's hand shot out and gripped Lana's arm. She felt like her arm had been caught in a rabbit snare. Her mother's fingernails bit into her skin, drawing a little blood. Before Lana could protest, her mother opened her mouth and howled a blood curdling scream, flecking her face with spittle which reeked of decay. It almost sounded like she was calling her name, though she couldn't be sure, her mind was frozen with fear.

With some effort, she managed to wrench her arm free from the vice-like grip. Amidst her panic, she noticed her mother hadn't budged an inch from all her pulling and shaking, which was surprising given the woman's small stature – Lana was a head taller than her. It was as though she was made of marble.

Finally free, she ran for the door tripping over a chair in the process sending her sprawling to the floor. She scrambled to her feet and sprinted out of the kitchen and down the hall without looking back.

She flew out of the front door in panic towards her father, screaming for his help. She stopped dead in her tracks just short of him. The man chopping wood wasn't her father any longer. It was the man in the black armour; the one wearing the huge gauntlet on his right hand.

Lana cried out in horror. He tilted his head at her, smiling; his teeth were vile and crooked. He gestured towards the pile of chopped wood. Lana looked down at the pile of wood. But it wasn't a pile of wood. It was human heads. Piles and piles of human heads. And not just any heads, she noticed, but her fathers' heads; dozens and dozens of them, all staring up at her.

She screamed once more. Her throat felt as though it was going to burst into flames at any moment. She tried to back away but her legs wouldn't move. The man in the black armour seemed to find her panic and pain very amusing, chuckling to himself.

"Silly child. Come here," he commanded, holding his hand out and flicking his fingers back towards himself.

Despite every fibre of her being protesting against the order, she felt her legs complying. She walked towards him.

He held out a hand, still smiling at her in an evil grin. Her legs stopped moving. She was only two feet away from him. She could smell his rancid breath and the stench of death emanating from him.

"Good girl," he said. "Now on your knees. Your insolence has left me with no other option. You must be punished."

She obeyed, falling to her knees without protest. Tears had begun to stream down her face. She looked back at the cottage. She was surprised to see her mother and father standing there on the porch, arm in arm, watching her. They were smiling, but the smiles were all wrong.

"Be a dear and bow your head for me," he said, sweetly. She complied.

After a few seconds of silence, she tilted her head up to face him, hoping to the Gods he'd gone. Her hope was in vain as she watched the axe as it was brought down onto her neck.

~

Lana shot bolt upright and screamed until she was breathless and shaking from head to toe.

Images of running through the forest flashed through her mind. Explosions going off all around. A bright light, and intense heat building within her then out of her. Falling through the air. Hitting cold water which embraced her in darkness. The face of a boy on the riverbank.

Then nothing.

She winced as a searing pain in her shoulder voiced its complaint breaking her from her reverie. She took in her current surroundings and didn't notice anything familiar. Where was she? She appeared to be lying in a soft bed in a strange room. Not her room though.

How did she get here? She rubbed at her eyes. She couldn't think. Her memories felt incomplete. There was so much missing; it came in flashes with breaks of nothing in between. She tried to think, rubbing her eyes a little harder. All that achieved was giving her little spots of light in her vision. Her home had been destroyed.

Then the reality of her situation hit her. She didn't have parents anymore. She lay back down and began to weep. After a while, it could have been ten minutes or ten hours for all she knew, she didn't care, she sat back up.

The room she was in was small; the bed took up the majority of the space, a small dresser sat underneath the window, and a bedside cabinet lay where its name intended.

She glanced over to the dresser and noticed her clothes were sitting on top of it in a neat pile. She pulled the bedsheets up and sighed with relief. She wasn't naked. She was wearing a nightdress a little too small for her, but at least she was wearing something. She guessed that whoever had brought her here had stripped, washed, and clothed her in her unconscious state, as she had no memory of it happening.

She also noticed the wound on her arm had been cleaned, and dressed in bandages – quite well, she thought. The dressings ran from her wrist up to her shoulder. She suddenly remembered being burned during her flight from the clearing. She touched her arm and winced as it was still tender.

She jumped as a knock at the door came from the other side of the door, followed by the sound of a familiar voice behind it. "Are you alright? I was in the yard and thought I heard someone screaming." The door opened a crack. "Can I come in?"

Whatever small irrational hope of this being another dream vanished as she recognised where she knew the voice from. It was the boy from the riverbank. "Yes, it's okay. You can come in," she said.

The door opened and the boy entered, carrying a tray laden with food; fresh bread, a plate of bacon and eggs – which made her mind think of the disturbing dream she'd had. There was also a steaming bowl of soup, and a couple of small cakes. Her stomach groaned. When had she last eaten? How long had she slept?

He put the tray down on the bedside

cabinet and retreated, taking a seat on the chair by the dresser. He waited quietly, looking out the window, as she wolfed down the bacon and eggs. The soup and cakes didn't last much longer either.

As she ate, her eyes never leaving the boy. He was small and wiry, his hair short and unkempt. He could have been twelve, maybe fourteen or fifteen at a push. It was hard to tell. He was younger than her, that was for sure. The shirt and hose he wore was a little dirty. She noted he had a kind face, with large brown eyes that shone from the sunlight coming through the window.

There seemed to be a nervousness to him, but she thought that might be due to him feeling a little self-conscious being near a girl a few years older than him, as she'd found with some of the boys she saw at the villages she and her father visited.

He put a hand on her folded clothes and turned to her. "I hope you don't mind, but mother insisted on changing you into one of her nightgowns." he said. She was glad it was only his mother that had seen her naked, she thought relieved. He continued. "She washed your clothes and mended as many of the burns as she could. She washed you too, and tended to that nasty cut on your shoulder, and the burn to your arm."

Lana reached to touch her bandaged shoulder absent-mindedly, then drew back as she remembered it was still sore. "Who are you?" she asked. "Where am I?"

The boy fidgeted in his seat and threw his arms up in the air. "I'm sorry...Yes, no, yes. Where are my manners," he stammered. Despite herself, she found him to be quite comical. "I'm Gren. I was fishing on the riverbank, just past where the river forks off towards Oakhaven. I found you lying underneath some driftwood on the riverbank. I thought you were dead... Then you weren't."

Lana shook her head. She rubbed her fingers against her temples, trying to remember. Only bits and pieces came to her. She remembered taking out her knife and...

"...I held a knife to your throat," she said, drawing a hand up to her neck. The colour on Gren's face told her as much as his cheeks began to turn red. She noticed a thin line no more than a few centimetres long marked his throat where her knife must have broken the skin.

He laughed nervously. "Yes, then you passed out. Lucky for me, eh?"

She felt ashamed. "I'm sorry I did that, Gren."

Gren got up and picked up the tray. "Don't worry about it. You've clearly been through a lot. Get some rest. When you're ready, come downstairs. We can talk if you want… when you're feeling more recovered. You can stay here for as long as you need."

"Gren," she said, before he left. He turned back around. "Thank you."

He smiled and left the room.

The warm food sitting in her full belly made her feel sleepy she realised. She lay back down and was asleep before the sound of Gren descending the stairwell had ceased.

Chapter Seven - The Wolf and the Tribesman

Kerr stopped his horse and looked back. The sun had begun to disappear behind the hills, casting a beautiful pink tinge to the evening sky. From its position, he guessed there would only be a couple more hours sunlight left. He patted his horse's neck and continued on, the mare kicking up a cloud of dust and dirt in its wake.

He'd spent the last week eating up the miles, putting as much distance between himself and Oakhaven. It left him with a lot to think about. A lot of loose ends he knew he'd have to answer for. He'd travelled north deciding against taking the most direct route to the temple – which was west of Oakhaven. After his disastrous parting with the king and the altercation at the inn he was certain the King, or Skallen at the very least, would send men after him.

He hadn't spotted a tail yet, though he wasn't naive enough to think there wouldn't be at some point, he fully expected it. All he could do was push on and hoped he reached the temple before they reached him.

Another thought constantly nagged at him. Grace; the barmaid from the inn. He hoped Banks hadn't found out she was the one who had tipped him off, for his sake. He thought about the kiss she'd gave him on the stairwell, surprised it brought a smile to his lips. Not all loose ends were unpleasant, he thought.

Just before it got too dark to ride any further, he found a spot to set up camp not far from a small stream, with a copse which would hide his presence from the road. He dropped down from his saddle and led his horse to the gentle flow of the stream. He patted her neck as she drank greedily. It had been a hard ride for his mount, of which he felt a little guilty. After the mare's thirst was sated, he hobbled her to a nearby tree, built a fire, and watched the rest of the sunset disappear for the day.

~

Kerr woke to the sound of a low growling coming from the copse not far from where he lay; a deep gravelling noise which made the hairs on his arms stand up on edge, leaving him in no doubt as to what made that particular sound. There was no mistaking the sound of a wolf when he heard one. His horse began to grow skittish – she whinnied and pulled at her bonds, sensing the predator.

Kerr remained where he was. He didn't want to make any sudden movements and draw attention to himself. He glanced up and around, but couldn't see much from his current position. Slowly, he reached down for his knife, finding comfort in the grip of its handle. He pulled it free from its scabbard and held it to his chest.

The wolf growled once more. It sounded like it had moved position, further away from him. Unfortunately, it was moving towards the horse. He carefully rolled onto his stomach and lifted his head up. He watched in horror as the biggest wolf he had ever seen slowly crept towards his horse, stalking low, its great bulk coiled like a spring.

He thought of his War-hammer, but it lay between the wolf and the horse. He looked disdainfully at the knife. He knew he had the skill to take the beast down with the blade. He just wasn't sure he'd be able to do it without taking at least one bite, and by the size of the big brute, that would probably be enough to kill him. His brows knitted together as he took in the sheer size of it. It was monstrous. Its head was nearly the same size as the horse's; a huge furred mass with a jaw that would be filled with teeth as big as his knife, and just as sharp.

It was getting closer to the mare; who was pulling at her bonds violently now.

The thought of carrying all his stuff the rest of the way spurred him out of his indecision and self-doubt. He rose to his feet, praying he was quiet enough and the beast too preoccupied with his horse. He was wrong. The wolf's ears pricked back in his direction. It turned its giant head and snarled at him; its teeth were a brilliant white in the moonlight.

He needed a new approach, he thought

ruefully. There was only one option open to him.

"Now, my friend," he said. "There's no need for undue sacrifice on both our parts."

He held his arms wide open and drew forth the power within him, deciding this method was more appropriate than the knife. He felt the old familiar tingling as his power grew. His hands began to glow faintly as he concentrated.

The wolf turned the rest of its body to face him. It was growling deeper and louder now, all thoughts of the horse gone from its mind. It padded towards him, its body language telling him it was ready to lunge at any moment.

Kerr shrugged at it. "Don't say I didn't warn you," he said, closing his eyes.

He still saw the wolf. His power had attuned his senses to an almost inhuman sensitivity. He had to time it right or he was finished. A small twitch from the wolf's shoulders gave him all the warning he needed.

As the wolf pounced for the kill, Kerr held out his hands in front of him. A blue transparent wall formed between him and the wolf. The wolf hit the wall with all its strength and weight behind it.

Unfortunately for the beast, the wall used this against it. It was held against the wall for no more than a second, sparks flew about from under it. It was blasted into the air then landed awkwardly into the stream.

Kerr watched as it went under the water. He wondered if it could swim. His question was answered as the wolf resurfaced and paddled to the opposite side of the stream. It reached dry land on the other side, shook itself quickly and ran with speed towards the woods, whining as it went.

"I didn't know you Knights could do that anymore," a voice said, behind him.

Kerr spun around, holding his blade up, and instinctively dropped into a battle stance. He immediately relaxed at the sight of his friend.

Judiah stood six and a half feet tall, his body looked like it had been carved from onyx stone – there wasn't an ounce of fat on the man he thought with a tinge of jealousy. He grinned down at him, the moonlight bouncing off his big bald head.

"How long have you been watching?" he asked, embracing the big man. To an onlooker, it probably looked like a little boy hugging his father, Kerr thought feeling a little self-conscious.

"The whole time, my friend," he said, chuckling. "I've been tracking that wolf you fired into the stream for most of the night." He pointed to where the wolf had disappeared into the forest.

Kerr sighed at him, exasperated. "And you didn't think to intervene? By the love of the Gods, Judiah. That thing could've ripped me to shreds."

Judiah threw his head back and laughed.

"You seemed to handle the situation well enough to me, my friend."

Kerr snorted at his friend. "Well I'll not be sleeping any time soon. Come, I'll get the fire going and we can talk for a time. Do me a favour, could you go over and calm the horse down. That monster of a thing gave her a fright."

While he built the fire, he told Judiah about his hasty departure from Oakhaven, and all the reasons for his sudden exodus. The big man nodded grimly as he patted and whispered to his horse, calming her.

After he was finished speaking, Judiah sat opposite him, remaining silent for a time while he digested the information. Kerr wrapped himself in a blanket waiting for the fire to grow large enough to give him a proper heat. Judiah never seemed to feel the chill. He wore only a thin shirt and a loin cloth. If anything, he looked quite hot. He surmised living high up on the mountains had something to do with it.

Eventually he leaned forward, his eyes boring into his. "I am sorry for your misfortune, Lord Knight, although not surprised by it," he said. Kerr leaned closer waiting for the big man to elaborate. "A great evil is growing. Our shamans have foreseen it. A fury is heading for these lands. It cares not for kings, or borders. Only malicious intent to enslave and butcher."

Kerr sighed. He respected Judiah and the Watalla. His father was Chieftain, Judiah his heir. Like the Hour, they didn't trust the true protection of the realms to kings and their nobles. They were too easily corrupted and manipulated. He just didn't buy into the fact there was a great and terrible evil coming. The High Lords would have been aware.

Although, seeds of doubt had begun to take root about his order. Was it possible they kept information such as this to a select few? He was growing concerned they may have lost their way. Grown complacent in peace-time.

Judiah looked at him with those deep penetrating eyes. He seemed to be able to read his thoughts. "Your doubts are not unjustified, my friend. The Knights of the Hour forgot who they were a long time ago. The old wars did not fully destroy the darkness like your predecessors thought. All it had to do was wait. Time can be a powerful weapon." Sometimes he found Judiah's gifts a little unnerving.

A weight felt like it had settled onto his shoulders. "When I find out what has happened at the temple. If the royal reports are true, and my brothers and sisters have fallen, we don't stand a chance. I'll be the last Knight of the Hour."

Judiah leaned forward once more. "Will you now?"

~

He spent the next week travelling further

north. His head swam with questions without answers. On the plus side, he didn't come across anymore wolves, or men from the palace hot on his trail. He had begun to guess the king may leave any repercussions until he returned, though with Skallen involved he couldn't be sure. That was something to look forward to, he thought sourly.

He thought back to the night Judiah had shared his camp. He'd been cryptic as his people usually were – telling their tales in riddles. "You aren't the last of your kind, my friend," he'd said. "The shamans have foretold it. They speak of the Fury being fought by men who harness the magic of their forefathers once more. They will aid the coming of the dawn."

Kerr had sat there, growing irritated at the accumulation of riddles. "What does that even mean, Judiah? The Fury? Is that a person? An army?" He'd stood and paced in front of the big man. "And the dawn? Does that mean the fighting only happens in the morning?"

Judiah had nothing to add in explanation to the meaning of his shaman's prophesy. "I don't hold the answers you seek, Lord Knight. As men, it is not our place to decipher the message, only to walk it's path and see where it takes us."

"That's ridiculous, Judiah. There's got to be a better way than that. How does that even work?"

Judiah had smiled at him. "I was told to seek you out. I asked the shaman where you would be found. He told me to follow the wolf." Kerr had nothing to add to that.

"And what did your shaman tell you to do when you found me?" he'd asked.

The big man had leaned forward. "To tell you, you are not alone. Continue with the path you walk. That the war will begin from the clearing."

He had woken to find the clansman had gone, which wasn't a shock. He suspected Judiah took great pleasure in being enigmatic. He knew his irritation was misplaced. It had vanished completely when he'd gone into his bag to find it had been stocked with a little food. Judiah was a good friend. Better than he deserved.

He slowed his horse to a canter as the city of Daltons Hill came into view. It sat within a U-bend the river had naturally created thousands of years ago. The lords keep sat on top of the hill the city derived its name from. He assumed it was built by a man named Dalton. It was surrounded by thick walls, and a deep moat, with a drawbridge at its front facing the river. Houses and fishermen's cottages were strewn all the way down the hill towards the harbour. He could see the many boats and cogs sailing in and out of it, rich with trade.

Two weeks of riding and sleeping rough had begun to make his joints sore. The thought of a soft feather bed and a decent ale sounded like just the thing he needed. The prospect of sleeping beneath a roof with a belly full of hot food and good ale raised his spirits. He urged his horse on in search of bread and board.

It didn't take him long to find a decent looking Inn. The proprietor of the 'Bay Trout' was a heavyset man with a huge beard that sat on a pronounced beer gut – affects from his own wares he had no doubt. The Innkeeper's eyes were drawn to the Warhammer clipped on his back.

"No rooms I'm afraid, Traveller," he said. A slight shake to his voice.

Kerr turned and took in the bar. Apart from a drunk, asleep on one of the tables near the back of the room, he was the only other patron. He turned back to face the Innkeeper. He dropped a handful of coins on the bar. The Innkeeper's eyes bulged at the wealth clattering about on his bar – and probably a little surprised at the lack of care from its owner.

"Could you check again?" he asked.

The Innkeeper didn't take his eyes from the coins as reached under the bar and produced a key. "You're in luck, traveller. One just became available. I'm Trevor, by the way. Owner of this fine establishment."

"How serendipitous, Trevor," he said, mocking a tone of shock and surprise.

Trevor collected the spilled coins in a neat pile and began to drag them towards the leather pouch around his waist. Kerr slammed a hand on top of it, causing Trevor to jump. He leaned forward, catching a waft of Trevor's breath, and wished he hadn't. "I presume my payment will include a hearty meal and a little ale, Trevor? I tell you, I'm famished, and I have a thirst you would not believe."

Kerr kept his hand over, the now sweating, Innkeeper's hand a little longer, enjoying the mixture of greed and fear that were fighting for dominance upon his face.

Trevor looked down at Kerr's robes, the realisation of a Knight of the Hour standing on the other side of his bar. "…Yes, my…my Lord. I'll send the girl up right away. Your room is upstairs, first one on the left."

Kerr patted the Innkeepers hand gently. "Good man." He winked and strode to the stairs feeling a little better than he had these last couple of weeks.

~

He opened the door and stepped into the small room; a desk and chair sat underneath the window, a bed against the wall to the right of it. It wasn't much. He regretted dropping so many coins onto Trevor's bar, but it would do for the one night. Besides, it was better than sleeping out in the open. More than a couple of occasions during his journey, he had woken up in the middle of the night to dislodge a rock he'd rolled onto in his sleep.

He unclipped his War-hammer from his back and slid it under the bed – it just fit and no more. He dropped his bag onto the floor and took a seat in the chair by the window. He kicked his boots off and sighed with relief. He wriggled his toes, which cracked in their own display of relief.

He looked out of the window, gazing at the view of the river from between two buildings across from the Inn. They were a little too close for his liking. He could make out a number of boats passing each other. Things would be a lot simpler if he were a fisherman. Spending every day in the fresh air. Maintaining the boat. Hiring a crew. Coming home to a family…

A knock at the door broke him from his daydream. "Enter," he said.

A young woman stepped in carrying a tray laden with hot bread, a jug of ale, and a steaming hot bowl of broth. His stomach rumbled at the sight and smell of the hot food, having spent the last two weeks being subjected to water and dried salted beef.

She put the tray down and lingered. "You need anything else Mi-Lord?" she asked in a husky voice. Her hand began to play with one of the braids in her hair. His gaze drifted down to her chest where a few of the top buttons had been undone revealing a generous amount of cleavage which looked like it was threatening to spill out and drop into his broth.

His tired mind finally caught up to what

she was offering – not just a waitress then.

He shook his head. "No, the food and ale will suffice."

She shrugged. "Suit yourself," she said, turned on her heels, and left him alone to his meal, slamming the door behind her.

The broth was good, though a little on the thin side. He wondered for a second if Trevor had spat in it, but he was too hungry to care, Trevor had been afraid of him so he doubted it. The bread was good; it was still warm in the middle as he tore chunks from it and dipped it into the broth. He drank the ale like a man who'd travelled the desert for weeks and finally come across water – which wasn't far from the truth. He began to feel its effects after the second mug-full. He was tempted to go downstairs and order another jug. No, he thought. Bad idea. Besides, he needed to keep a clear head.

He got up and half stumbled onto the bed, where he lay back and fell asleep, not bothering to undress.

~

He was woken to the sound of thumping coming from the other side of his door. At first, he'd thought it was coming from inside his head. It was followed by a gruff voice. "Open this door, in the name of Lord Cunningham, Duke of these lands."

Not a good start to the day.

He sat up with a groan, and took his time

putting his boots on – he'd make this pompous idiot wait. The door thumped once more, a little louder this time. "Open this door, or I shall be forced to fetch the Innkeeper to open it for me."

Right, now he was annoyed. Kerr opened the door halfway through the next volley of knocks. "And do what?" he growled.

Standing in front of him was a man dressed in armour that looked as though it had never seen live combat in its life. Lord Cunningham's seal was emblazoned on the chest-plate; an eagle with a trout in its beak. He presumed Lord Cunningham would think himself the eagle, he thought, chuckling inwardly.

The rapid opening of the door, and his aggressive tone seemed to have caught the guard off guard – ironic, he thought, amused. The man quickly recovered his composure, and began to unroll a piece of parchment. Kerr didn't need to hear the bluster from some jumped up messenger boy with disillusions of grandeur to know what a Lord's summons looked like

"Tell your Lord I'll be up to his keep within the hour," he said, slamming the door in the guard's face. He listened as the guard muttered to himself, footsteps thumping down the hallway and down the stairs. He chuckled as he gathered his belongings and left the room.

The guard was standing at the end of the bar when he entered. Kerr smiled as he passed Trevor. He tossed the key to him, which he failed to catch, and had to scuffle about on the floor to find it.

"I shall escort you to the keep," the guard said.

"Not if you like your teeth where they are, you won't," Kerr replied, not looking back.

Chapter Eight - Royal Wine and Dragon Root

The palace was quiet save for the sound of cutlery being laid out, or the echoed footsteps of the servants as they finished preparing the various rooms for the next day's proceedings. Candles were lit along the corridors, their light shimmering off the armour of the guards standing vigil at the many doors and entrances throughout the building.

At the top of the central tower, standing several floors higher than the rest of the palace, were the royal bed-chambers. King Hal was inside. He lay on the royal bed, feeling content with himself as the breeze from the open window washed over his naked flesh, a welcome sensation after the rigorous lovemaking he'd enjoyed with his wife. He watched as Isabel got up from their bed and walked over to the dresser. Beads of sweat glistened the contours of her body as she poured herself a goblet of wine and drank deeply.

"Thirsty, my dear?" he asked playfully, still a little breathless from their exertions.

She turned, her golden hair swishing around and settling over her shoulder. Gods she was beautiful, he thought. She raised an eyebrow at him. "Why yes, my love. It's thirsty work performing Queenly duties for her King." She took another sip, then curtsied. He bowed his head to her.

Maybe this time, he thought. Maybe this was the time he planted a seed in her womb. She would give him the heir he'd been desperate for, ensuring his bloodline lived on. He would have his dynasty.

They'd been married for ten years, and attempts of producing an heir had so far proven fruitless. Over the course of the decade, they had procured the help from the best medical minds in the realm to aid in their efforts. Unfortunately, none of them had succeeded.

"Would you be able to serve your King once more, and bring him a glass of wine?" he asked. Wine was always good after their lovemaking. He had a variety of the finest vintages in the world sitting on his dresser. He could go weeks without having two glasses of the same vintage.

"Of course, your Grace."

She poured a glass and approached the bed, he took in all of her curves as they swayed towards him. She handed him the glass, smiling as he drank his fill, savouring the rich grape as it slid down his throat. They then lay in silence for a while, enjoying each other's company.

She rolled onto her side, facing him. "What's wrong Hal? Tell me what troubles you?" she asked.

He sighed. Even after all these years she still surprised him with her ability to read him like an open book. "The ugly business with the Knight. I feel I lost my temper and acted rashly, said things I didn't really mean. My temper got the better of me. I should have silenced that brother of mine. He stepped over the line."

"You are a King, my love. Your concern for the safety of your subjects may have taken precedence over events at the temple. Your brother was only protecting his King's rule."

He shook his head. "That's the point though, Izzy, my father taught me a King should act with a level head. Especially in his own court. He doesn't hide behind his noblemen for protection," he said, exasperated. He could feel his chest tightening. He took a deep breath.

Isabel sat up and placed a hand onto his. "You act out of passion, my love." She slid her other hand onto his chest, curling the dark hairs around her slender fingers. "It's one of the many reasons why I fell in love with you."

He smiled up at her. She had the most mesmerizing eyes he'd ever seen; a dark brown tinged with a hint of red. He glanced down at her chest as it rose and fell; goosebumps covered her pale skin from the chill coming in from the window.

"I should have been more sensitive. The man is now alone in the world. The Hour is gone, according to Skallen's reports. This is going to cause issues once King Richard hears the news, that is if he wasn't the one responsible." His chest began to tighten once more. He finished his glass in one long draught.

Isabel took the empty glass, and walked back to the dresser to refill it. "When he returns, I have faith you will do the right thing. Trust me." She glided back towards him, her hips swaying demurely, and handed him the glass. He took another mouthful.

"Yes, I will make it right when he returns." He sighed, breathing normally once more – though the tightness remained.

"You will because you're a good man." She bent down and picked up her nightgown, which had been roughly discarded in the heat of their coupling, and put it back on. "You know, I heard an interesting piece of knowledge from one of the ladies of the court. Lord Arnold's wife, Lady Elizabeth. They have just returned from their estates near the mountains."

He lay his head back and listened to his wife, hoping it would take his mind from recent events. And the tightening of his chest. Was it getting worse? He looked up at his wife as she was telling her story. She seemed not to notice his growing discomfort.

She continued. "They held court up there with a rather interesting man. One of the leaders from the mountain clans, which I thought was interesting as they are usually so reclusive.

They got to talk a little on their healing methods. You know how I'm interested in the healing arts." He was half listening now.

He was beginning to struggle with each breath he took. It felt like a cow was sitting on his chest.

"There's a sickness of the lungs which causes fitting, the patient also has trouble breathing." She held up the glass she'd been holding. "Did you know there is a particular type of plant that can ease the patients suffering? The mountain clans call it the Dragon Root. They can be so dramatic when naming things, I think," she said, giggling.

He tried to raise his arm. He wished she would stop prattling on and notice he was struggling to breath.

Still she continued. "You grind the root into a fine powder, and put a pinch in their water. Just a pinch. Within minutes, their breathing returns to normal. It's really quite extraordinary."

His breathing was coming in laboured rasps now. If she knew how to ease his suffering with this damn root...

"Here's the bit you'll find most interesting of all," she said, putting her glass down. "Say someone didn't use a pinch, but put two spoonsful of the powder in the patient's water, do you know what would happen to them?" She paused a moment, staring at him as he struggled. "Yes, you guessed it. The complete opposite. I won't bore you with the details of how that would turn out. Just now, I think you know better than anyone."

She smiled a smile he'd never seen before. It was horrible. There was no joy to be found in it, only spite, and hate, and malice. Her eyes gleamed with rage. In his incapacitation, he managed to whimper 'why'.

"Why?" she shrieked. "Why? Because you're a petty little man playing at being King. Because you haven't the vision to see what this kingdom needs. It needs a true leader. It needs the Knights of the Hour gone so we can move forward into a new world. A world that isn't split in two. A world that has only one King."

She slowly approached the bed he was writhing on. He could feel his throat close completely finally shutting off the air supply to his burning lungs. She got on her knees and whispered into his ears the last words he'd ever hear. "But most of all, my love, because you couldn't give me a son."

He stared back at her. His eyes vacant, but for a single tear that had begun to roll down his cheek. He was dead.

"Is he dead?" a voice called out from the shadows in the corner of the room.

Isabel leapt onto her dead husband's chest, straddling him. She slapped his face a few times, feeling ten years of frustration leaving her with every swipe. Once she was satisfied, she turned. "The great oaf is dead."

Skallen approached and looked down at his brother. "Believe it or not, I did love the big fool once. I can't quite place when it stopped, but I did at some point," he said. Isabel stared at him from atop his brother.

"You can get off him now, my dear."

She looked down at her husband, and kissed his forehead. She didn't bother closing his eyes. "I will miss the lovemaking. He was rather good. I think that was the reason why I kept him alive for so long." She rolled off him and stood next to Skallen, who raised an eyebrow at her.

"You know the real reason it had to wait until now, Izzy," he said, dryly.

She whirled on him, pointing a finger at him. "Don't call me that," she hissed. "I had to put up with that idiot calling me that for years. I'm well aware of why it had to be now." She took a step back. "Now get on with it."

"As my Queen commands," Skallen said, as he punched her in the jaw, sending her clattering into the dresser. Bottles of rare wines, antique glasses and goblets smashed onto the floor. She crawled over to the mirror on her wardrobe, cutting herself multiple times in the process. Her lip had begun to bleed, and a bruise was forming where he'd struck her. It throbbed in great pulses.

She spat a mouthful of blood, and rose to her feet. "That won't do. Again."

He grabbed her by the hair and smashed her face against the mirror, which shattered. He kept a grip of her locks, holding her legs upright and struck her again. She dropped to the floor unmoving.

He bent down and checked she was still

breathing. She was. When they'd discussed their plan earlier, he'd been strongly against striking her. She'd waved his reluctance aside and told him it was necessary.

He pulled a dagger from its sheath, and approached the King.

~

The palace bells could still be heard from within the interior council chambers, despite the heavy doors being closed, as the lords waited for news of their monarch and his queen. The hall was filled with a mixture of fear and disbelief, having heard only snippets of information.

All heads turned as the doors opened, and Skallen, Lord Commander of the royal forces, entered with an entourage of military aids. The noblemen gave a wide berth to the King's brother as he made his way up to the podium.

He climbed the steps and turned to face them, his face taut with anger and grief. Their chatter ceased. "My Lord's, I've called you here, at this ungodly hour, as I bear terrible news." He paused, a frown forming on his brow. The room was as quiet as a crypt. "Our great King has been slain. Murdered in his own chambers."

The room exploded with shouts, and questions, and cries of outrage. He held up a hand, and gestured to one of his aids to step forward. The soldier was carrying something wrapped in cloth. "The King was overpowered and killed trying to protect the Queen from a vicious assault on her person."

"Who would attack our beloved queen? What madness is this?" Lord Arnold demanded, stepping forward. "Is the Queen alive?"

"My Lords, give thanks to the Gods, our Queen is recovering in her rooms. If it wasn't for the selflessness of my brother..." He paused, grimacing. "Who knows what could have happened to her. Luckily a servant heard the commotion coming from the royal chambers, and alerted the guards."

"What of the assassin, Lord Commander? Was the Queen his target, or the King?" Lord Arnold asked.

Skallen shook his head. "According to the Queen's account of events, before she was taken away by the physician to have her wounds tended to, the killer escape through the window."

He ordered the aid to open the wrappings. He complied and handed Skallen a dagger. "Without a suspect in our custody, we can only deduce the King, and the Queen, were both his targets."

He held the dagger aloft. "Our King was stabbed through the heart with this."

Further cries filled the hall. He ordered another aid to come forward. The soldier approached the Commander, bearing another item. He handed it over to Skallen. "During his escape, the assassin's cloak snagged on the window ledge, he was forced to leave it behind lest he be captured by the guards." He held the cloak up for all to see. "I think you'll all agree, my Lords, it provides us with enough evidence to surmise where the source of the assassination has come from."

Across it's back, the cloak bore the sigil of the Knights of the Hour.

Chapter Nine - Lord Cunningham's Keep

Kerr arrived at Lord Cunningham's keep just after noon, three hours later than he'd said to the toady who had woken him earlier. Deliberately taking his time, he'd spent the morning browsing the many stalls in the market quarter which, in his defence, was situated on the other side of the building opposite the Inn. He was tailed the entire time by the pedantic guard. The horrible little man obviously valued his teeth, as he wisely kept his distance.

Once he'd finished purchasing supplies for the journey ahead, he'd began to slowly climb up the steep hill towards the keep, deciding to guide his horse by the reins instead of riding her – the street was too busy to be galloping up on horseback. Not long after he'd started his assent, the muscles in his thighs began to burn in protest.

He marvelled at the way the houses he passed sat on the hill; huddled together making the most of the space they shared. Whoever the architect had been, they'd known their craft on building solid houses on steep hills. While he struggled, the residents, some pulling carts full of goods, didn't seem to share his toil. The sweat soon began to stream down his face. More than a couple smiled as they passed. With his audible panting, he may as well have held up a sign that read 'Outsider'.

He was certain his tail wasn't far behind him, probably finding his obvious struggle with the hill amusing. He didn't turn around. He wasn't giving him the satisfaction of seeing his face, which he suspected was as red as a fresh summer strawberry.

He stopped short of the bridge which crossed the moat to catch his breath. He looked up at the ramparts above the arched entrance to the main courtyard. Four crossbowmen stood guard; they glanced down at him coldly as he caught his breath. There was probably several more behind them he couldn't see.

He crossed the bridge and passed under the arch. The courtyard was busy with servants and soldiers carrying out their duties. The grounds were covered in rushes that looked as though they were replaced regularly. No-one gave him a sideways glance as he led his horse to the foot of the steps that led into the keep. His mare hadn't even broken out in a sweat from the climb, much to his annoyance.

A stable-boy approached him and took the reins of his horse, promising she would be fed, watered, and brushed when he came back out. He flipped the boy a gold coin with his thanks.

He climbed the steps where two guards blocked his path, bearing cruel looking pikes.

"We'll have to relieve you of your bag

and weapon, my Lord," one of them said, sternly.

Kerr handed over his bag to one of them, unclipped his War-hammer and gave it to the one who had spoken. The guard, not realising the huge weapon had been bound by magic making it lighter for its owner, just about dropped to the floor with it. He was impressed he managed to stay upright.

"Careful," he said, winking at him. "You don't want to hurt yourself."

"In there," the guard said, curtly, choosing not to react to his jibe – a disciplined soldier, he thought, you didn't come by them very often. Kerr nodded, respecting the soldier a little more, and entered the keep.

He strolled down the long corridor which presumably led to Lord Cunningham's audience chambers. Huge portraits of Daltons Hill's past lords lined the walls on either side. They were fitted onto golden frames crafted into intricate designs clearly displaying the wealth Cunningham's family had enjoyed over the generations.

He reached the end of the hall to a massive oak door. A soldier opened it using a leaver to one side. He heard mechanical cogs grinding behind the door frames as the doors opened. The guard beckoned him to enter.

Lord Tallon Cunningham sat on a garish throne at the opposite end of the room. He had a goblet of wine in hand; the glass almost completely covered by his chubby fingers – sausages suddenly sprang to his mind.

"Ah, Lord Kerr, I was beginning to worry you had gotten lost, I was on the verge of sending a search party," he said, flourishing his free hand in a mock regal wave. A little wine spilled over the goblet and onto his shirt, he seemed not to notice. "Did you plan on passing through my city without visiting it's Lord? I must admit I am disappointed. I thought you knights held tradition in high esteem?"

Kerr approached, passing under a great chandelier high above his head, glittering with countless number of jewels and sapphires. The room was circular in shape. He noticed there were several guards stationed around it's outer wall; armed with short swords sheathed at their waists.

"Only the traditions that matter, my Lord. You had your loyal man summon me for an audience. Here I am," he said, dryly.

Cunningham leaned forward. "Yes, here you are. Two hours later than expected." He got up from the chair and walked down the stone steps – swaying a little, he noticed. Kerr wondered how many cups he'd had before the current one.

Kerr chose to speak first, and get the 'audience' over with. "May I enquire as to the nature of your summons? You see, as you've no doubt heard, my home is reportedly lying in a state of ruin, with my brothers and sisters put to the sword. So, with all due respect, I would like to be on my way."

Cunningham waved a hand, dismissing the comment – and not seeming too heartbroken about his Order's supposed destruction. "I am well aware of your Order's sad state of affairs, Knight. My personal scouts aided Lord Skallen in his investigations."

Cunningham drained his goblet, and refilled it from a nearby drinks tray whose, Kerr suspected, location was not an accident. He did not offer Kerr a cup as was customary to do when holding court with a guest. So much for tradition.

Kerr ignored the obvious slight. "You don't seem too concerned about the Hour's misfortunes. I presume you share Lord Skallen's scorn for me and my kind?"

"I couldn't care less if I'm being honest, Knight. There are more important matters to be dealing with than the goings on of your secretive order. Haven't you heard? There will be war soon."

Kerr was losing what little patience he had left. He'd be damned to the fiery hells if he was going to stand here and have his order disrespected by this bloated drunk.

Cunningham was oblivious to his guest's growing anger. He began to pace back and forth, as though in a deep philosophical thought process. Kerr surmised his alcohol addled mind was struggling to keep up with the conversation. He suddenly stopped as though a great idea had come to him. He turned to face him. "You say Lord Skallen? Don't you mean King Skallen?"

The news hit him like a punch to the guts. He spluttered his disbelief. Cunningham's face failed to hide the delight in being the first to break the news of the King's death. "The King is dead? How? When?" He barely got the words out. King Hal was dead.

"A week ago. An assassin broke into the royal bedchambers and brutally assaulted the Queen." He shook his head. "The King managed to fight back, defending his beloved wife. But his assailant... no, murderer, somehow managed to overpower him, which is surprising given the size of his Grace."

His thoughts were now a jumble of questions. He was beginning to have trouble getting his wits in order. "How is the Queen? Will she recover?" He hoped she would. She was Grunald's rock. The rock to King Hal's steel.

Cunningham gave him a look of deep sadness and concern – it didn't suit him. "In time, her injuries will heal. Although it may take her Grace longer to recover from her mental trauma. She's been locked in her rooms ever since. She'll see no-one except her handmaidens and King Hal's brother."

Kerr felt a mixture of grief and guilt. They had parted on ill terms. He would make amends to the Queen when he returned to Oakhaven – though he wouldn't be surprised if she threw his apologies back in his face. Also, going back to a city where Skallen was king, didn't fill him with much enthusiasm.

Despite his doubts on the outcome of his return, he felt he owed it to King Hal's memory. "I will return," he said. "But after I have travelled to the temple to see for myself if it has been destroyed. I owe it to my brethren."

Cunningham looked almost disappointed, the way a father looked at an unruly son. Kerr gritted his teeth, almost failing to succumb to the urge of breaking the Lord's nose in front of his soldiers. "There is currently an investigation to ascertain the nature of the assassination, and the attempt on the Queen's life. I strongly advise you head back the way you came and aid in their efforts... isn't that what you Knights are supposed to do? To come to the realm's aid in times of need."

Kerr didn't need lessons of the Hour's purpose from this bloated worm. Though some of what he'd said made sense, he would have believed it if were not for the amount of guards stationed in the room. A little too many for a meeting between two men.

It was possible Skallen may have known Kerr wouldn't travel west from Oakhaven, but instead north to throw off a pursuit. Also, Cunningham hadn't enquired to his unusual choice of direction from the capital to the temple either, which he found odd. A raven could have been sent by Skallen to Cunningham, warning him of the possibility of a Knight of the Hour passing through his lands. Kerr would have done the same thing if he were in Skallen's shoes. As much as he disliked Skallen, he was a military man known and respected for his skills in strategy.

The more he thought about it, the more it made sense. Something was at play here. Something bigger than Cunningham – the man was slippery, but had all the cunning of a boiled potato. Cunningham no doubt knew of Kerr's ill-mannered departure from Oakhaven. If that was the case, he was sure Skallen would command his Lord to 'persuade' Kerr to return.

He took a step closer to Cunningham, he noticed a couple of guard's tense at the move towards their Lord. "And if I refuse?" he asked.

Fear flickered over the Lord's face, which he quickly recovered. He waved a hand, and gave a nervous chuckle. "It matters not what you do, Knight. Don't heed my council, see where it gets you." He narrowed his eyes at the Knight. "Though some may find your refusal to return to the capital suspicious, given the timing of your flight, and the death of the King."

Kerr had had enough of the pompous Lord's games. In two quick strides, he was on the Lord. He grabbed him by the throat, and lifted him in the air. Cunningham dropped the goblet which shattered, spilling its contents onto the stone floor His eyes bulged in surprise at Kerr's strength, his feet dangling a foot above the floor.

The guards rushed forward, crossbows aimed at his head. "You will drop our Lord, in the name of the King," one of them commanded.

Kerr didn't take his eyes off the Lord he held aloft. He wasn't worried about the guards, he'd summoned a shield before he'd taken his first step. "Are you making an accusation, my Lord?" He spat the title out like it was bile. "I'm growing tired of the games being played at my expense. No-one seems to understand what is going on. If what I find is true, the consequences will be bigger than this kingdom or its politics."

Despite being held off the ground by his neck, Cunningham managed to speak. "I understand perfectly well, Knight. Now put me down before my men put you down."

Kerr held him where he was for a moment longer. He was sorely tempted to scatter the room with Cunningham, and his men. The constant lack of care and disregard for his order disturbed and angered him. Feeling his rage turn to weariness, and a sudden urge to remove himself from the city of Daltons Hill, he dropped the Lord onto his backside. He coughed and retched, taking in deep breaths, his hands rubbing his throat.

The Lord looked up at him with a burning hatred from his watery eyes. The soldiers closed in, surrounding him.

Kerr took in each of them in a measured look. "I'm ready when you are, boys," he said, flatly.

They stood for a moment, in a stand-off, each side waiting for the other to make the first move. It was Cunningham who broke the silence that had descended upon the chambers. "Stand down. Leave us. Go Knight, be gone from my keep, and my lands. You're not welcome here any longer."

Kerr laughed in spite of the severity of his current predicament. "I was welcome? Lord Cunningham, you could have fooled me."

He left the keep, his footsteps echoing as he went, with Lord Cunningham still on his ass, staring in his wake.

~

Argon had watched the meeting from the shadows with great fascination. This Knight could be trouble if left unchecked. He wasn't worried. He would be dealt with in time. He was a patient man, he had learned a long time ago to avoid rash moves if it could be helped.

He watched as Cunningham dismissed his guards, getting up onto his feet with all the grace of a rutting pig. He felt nothing but scorn towards the Lord. He was a self-important fool, unaware he was merely a cog in the great machine. A pawn with delusions of grandeur, which made him blind to his own insignificance in the events to come. He will come to realise it by the end...they all will, he thought, a smile pulling at his lips.

He glanced in the direction this Lord Kerr had gone with his remaining eye; the other a ruined mass of scar-tissue. It seemed he wasn't as informed on the Order's movements as he'd first thought. A Knight in the capital? That was a surprise. He wondered if there was one stationed in Helven's capital; Stonewatch. It was something that needed looking into. They were weeds that needed to be pulled. If left unchecked they could strangle their plans in its infancy.

There was the girl too, the one from the clearing. He'd raged at his lieutenants when they had returned from their pursuit of her empty handed. They had explained in great detail the nature of her escape. They assured him the cliff had been high, the river wild, that she'd most probably died from the fall.

His mind still lingered on her. He'd seen the light through the tree's, from the direction of her flight. At first, he'd assumed one of his men had struck true with one of his missiles, burning her to ash.

If the light had come from her, that could mean...? The Dawn? He shook his head dismissing the thought. It didn't matter what his men said to convince him she had perished. He wouldn't leave the issue without a body.

His patience and persistence had been wise. He knew where she was, having received word from one of his many agents, scattered throughout the realm. She'd been found, half dead, washed up on the riverbank by a local boy. She'd been taken to their home, which resided within Lord Cunningham's city borders.

He watched as the last of the guards left, closing the oak doors behind them, leaving Lord Cunningham alone to drown his injured pride in more wine. Quiet as a shadow, he crept up behind him and whispered in his ear. "You did well, my Lord."

To his satisfaction, Cunningham just about jumped out of his skin. He stumbled forward, almost toppling over his precious drinks' cabinet. He whirled around with a look of fear – presumably thinking the Knight had returned – which turned to annoyance at the sight of Argon standing in front of him.

"Hells bells, Argon, must you sneak up on a man like some snake in the night..." He stopped, his gaze drawn to his ruined eye. "What on earth happened to your eye?"

"That's exactly what I am, my Lord. A snake in the night, for I need to be if things are to progress the way they are supposed to." He touched his eye. "This is just another mark of my self-sacrifice in the wars to come. Something you know nothing of."

Cunningham snorted derisively. He pointed to the oak doors. "My guards could have just killed that arrogant knight and be done with it. My men had him surrounded."

Argon shook his head. He was clearly unaware of his own arrogance. "Do you really think your men could have taken down a Knight of the Hour? Surrounded or not? He would have killed them, then you, unarmed in under a minute."

Cunningham rolled his eyes. "I think you've been listening to too many of the children's stories, about the mythical knights who fought demons and monsters. They are men, flesh and blood, just like you and me. We have armies at our beck and call. What can one knight, now without a home, do to us?"

Argon seethed with rage at the fool's ignorance. The kingdom was rife with men like Cunningham. Thankfully in the very near future it would be a thing of the past. At the moment, unfortunately, they were a necessary evil that had to be endured.

It didn't mean they couldn't be brought to heel.

Argon's hand shot out and gripped Cunningham's throat. Twice in the space of a matter of minutes, he was not having a good day. He pulled the Lord towards him, their noses almost touching. "Events stand on a house of cards, my Lord. They will not be hindered by some petty little nobleman who acts above his station."

He threw Cunningham back, sending him sprawling onto the floor. He pointed a chubby finger in Argon's direction, but remained on the floor. "How dare you treat me in this manner, Captain. The King shall hear of this. I will not be disrespected."

It was an empty threat. Skallen hated the man as much as he did. Argon smiled down at the fool. "Then act like a Lord and not some petty child."

He climbed the steps and took a seat in Cunningham's horrible looking chair. Cunningham looked as though he was about to protest, then thought better of it. "The Knight will be dealt with accordingly. It is of no concern to you. I have another task you may prove of some use."

Cunningham got up, and dusted himself off. "And what would that be?" he asked sarcastically.

Argon leaned forward. "My men and I were hunting enemies of the crown, a couple of weeks ago, in the depths of the great forest. We apprehended and dealt with them all...except one. A girl, no more than twenty years old, dark hair, very pale but pretty. She managed to escape our custody. She had used the river to slip through our fingers. I enquired on her whereabouts in every village and town on my way here. No-one had seen her.

That was until one of my scouts reported she had been found by one of your residents. Found upstream, and half dead. Tell me, my

Lord, do I have reason to doubt my agent? Have you heard of a girl found by the riverbank?"

Lord Cunningham smiled, telling Argon all he needed to know. He didn't really need the Lord's help. He would have been able to find her within his city on his own. Sometimes though, to keep a Lord onside – especially one who's loyalty was subject to who had the better offer – it was good to make them feel they contributed to the cause.

He needed Cunningham's fighting men. Unfortunately, Cunningham came along with it.

"Yes, a girl was found a couple of weeks ago, by one of my tenants, a farmer... no, his son. Greg, or Grif, the boy's name was, I think. He brought her to his father's cottage, on the outskirts of the city. A small patch of farmland near the edge of the forest. Will I send my men to apprehend her?"

Argon smiled, showing plenty of teeth. "No, my Lord. Soon. I will keep an eye on her. I have something special planned for that girl." He wasn't worried about her disappearing again, she had nowhere to go. He would bide his time.

After all, he was a patient man.

Chapter Ten - Sparring Practice

It had been three weeks since Gren had found Lana on the riverbank. For the first two, she'd barely left her room; on the few occasions she had, she'd quickly returned, usually in a flood of tears, with his mother following in her wake.

Gren's mother, June, had spent the most time with her. She'd cleaned and redressed her wounds, and provided a shoulder to cry on when her grief from losing her parents had been too much to bear. His mother hadn't pressed her for information, for fear of upsetting her, of causing her to relive whatever had happened to her. She'd simply told her it would get easier with time.

The nightmares that had plagued Lana since she'd arrived at their home had provided a little information. She sometimes cried out in her sleep, as though she was still there.

From what they could gather she had witnessed her parents murder at the hands of mysterious men wearing black armour. She was then chased, where she'd fell into the river from a cliff-top. If it was true, Gren was amazed she had survived, the fall into the river should have killed her.

His mother had asked about the group of men wearing the black armour just the once during the first week. Lana had clammed up, refusing to speak for two days. Gren suspected part of the reason was that she didn't fully trust her erstwhile carers, which was understandable.

He looked up at her window. He was standing in the yard. It was a warm day, and with his mother cooking, the house had felt stuffy. He'd asked his mother if he could take Lana's meal up to her when it was ready. She refused, telling him the sudden change in their routine could upset her. He felt his mother was bordering on the overbearing, but he chose not to press the issue.

An image of Lana on top of him surfaced unexpectedly in his mind. He shivered at the thought. He wasn't particularly big for his age, if anything he was on the short side. Nevertheless, he'd been surprised by the strength in her. The way she'd thrown him to the ground as though he weighed no more than a bag of flour. Where had she come from to know how to do that?

He shook the thought aside, and returned his gaze to the makeshift practice block he'd brought out the moment his father had left for market. His father would have a fit if he knew what Gren did every time he went to the city. He held the strong opinion Gren would be a farmer, not a soldier. Gren somewhat disagreed.

He picked up the crudely made practice sword; two pieces of wood nailed together, the tips of the nails sheared away so as not to cut himself. He began to swipe at the block, mimicking the stances and practice methods used by Lord Cunningham's personal guard. In his free time, he would sneak up to the practice yard, with his friend Marissa, to watch the soldiers spar, taking down mental notes of their positioning, and sword techniques. Looking down at his poor excuse for a practice blade, he knew swinging a stick at a block he'd made in his back garden would only get him so far. Not very far at that.

He would choose the right time to broach the subject with his father, though it didn't fill him with hope. Any time he'd managed to find the courage to bring up the courage to mention it was quickly dashed the minute he made eye-contact with his father. His father had visions of him taking over the farm when he retired, and raising a family of his own. It was a nice thought. But it wasn't for him. He wanted the life of a soldier, defending the realm from the King's enemies. They weren't at war so it would be against roving bandits and criminals – that suited him fine.

News of the King's murder had spread through the city like wildfire. Supposedly killed defending the Queen, who'd been seriously injured and was recovering in her royal apartments. His brother, Skallen, was now king on account of there being no heir. It hardly affected the way of life for himself, being a lowly farmers son. But he found it interesting as grim as it was. It made his life on the farm that little bit duller.

Losing himself in his practice, he began to swing the sword in wide arcs, crossing over from time to time. It was the style fashioned by the guard. Just as he was getting into his rhythm, something hit him on the back, followed by the sound of familiar voices.

"Hey Gren, where's your girlfriend?" Finn asked, vaulting the fence.

"He's probably got her locked in his room. It's the only way he can keep a piece of skirt." Tom said, following his friend.

Gren felt his cheeks redden in spite of himself. Why couldn't they just leave him alone? "What do you want?" he asked, his eyes narrowing.

"Come to see the expert swordsman of course," he said, smirking at Gren's practice sword. He pulled his own, a real one, from its scabbard. He held it up, the sunlight reflecting off it's polished surface. "Now this, Gren, is a sparring blade."

He twirled it in intricate swings and twists. The sparring blades used up at the practice yard were made of steel. They were blunted so as not to kill – it was hardly solace if you were struck with one, which he suspected was about to happen. In the end it was still a length of hard, unforgiving steel.

Finn stopped just short of Gren, and took a mock bow. "Think you can take me?"

Before Gren could reply, Finn lunged at him. Taken unawares he made a pathetic attempt to block Finn's attack. His practice sword was easily swatted aside, leaving him open to receive a strike to his upper arm which sent a jolt of pain shooting down his arm, numbing it.

He quickly backtracked, fully expecting Finn to follow up the hit. He didn't however, choosing to boast to his friend instead. Tom applauded, clapping like an idiot. As he rubbed his aching arm, he wondered if Tom asked Finn's permission to use the privy.

"Now Tom, like we discussed earlier after practice, the best way to approach a duel is to begin with speed and aggression, striking fear into the heart of your opponent." He swung the blade around, displaying his skill. "Then hold back a moment, giving your opponent a false sense of security. Make him think you're not sure how to proceed with the rest of the fight."

He quickly turned and lunged at Gren once more. This time Gren was ready for the attack. He parried the first riposte, dodged a second which merited a look of surprise from the big brute. Finn narrowed his eyes, and swung at Gren once more. They traded a few more blows; five from Finn, and a clumsy one from himself.

As their sparring match lingered on, Gren began to grow in confidence. He was doing it. Holding his own – mostly – against a boy who was currently under tuition from the drillmasters at the Lord's keep.

He caught a smirk from Finn which

turned his confidence to dust. He realised then he was being toyed with. He should have known. Build him up then knock him down. It was certainly Finn's style. Finn could have knocked him on his ass at any moment.

How could he think training once a week in his backyard, with no tutor, and a stick for a sword made him a match against a trainee of the Lord's personal guard?

Stupid. Stupid. Stupid.

His realisation proved true as Finn easily dodged a clumsy thrust, sidestepped another, and in a blur of sudden speed dealt Gren a series of blows. He was struck twice on the thighs, then his stomach, doubling him over. He barely had time to react to them before the flat of Finn's blade came rushing up to meet him. His mouth exploded in white hot pain as he was thrown back, landing hard on his back, biting his tongue in the process.

His vision blurred. He could taste copper in his throbbing mouth. He was aware of a groaning sound, which he soon realised was coming from his own mouth. He managed to sit up. His head felt like a sack of flour poorly balanced upon his shoulders. Through the fog of what he knew would be a cracked skull, he could see Finn and Tom growing smaller and smaller as they left, victorious. A voice called back to him, he presumed it was Finn.

"Stick to farming, Gren. Leave the soldiering to your betters," Finn shouted.

He looked down at himself. Some victory.

He remained where he was for a time, all the while feeling an even mixture of anger and self-loathing. For some reason he glanced up at Lana's window.

Had the curtains just moved?

~

He spent the rest of the afternoon making repairs to his boat. It kept his mind active, and off his disastrous spar with Finn – if you could call it that, more like an assault. His bottom lip had swollen on one side, he could feel it pressing against his teeth.

His mother and, surprisingly, Lana were sitting at the kitchen table when he eventually ventured back inside. Lana had given him a sympathetic smile which he couldn't return – on account of his bottom lip doing a pretty good impression of a slug. His mother had asked him what had happened to his lip.

"I lost control of the hammer mending one of the fence posts," he'd lied. His mother wasn't stupid, she just chose not to press the issue.

"I've heard those fences can be dangerous if left untended," Lana had said, her lips like slits, those pale blue eyes penetrating into his own.

He'd left without another word, feeling Lana's gaze at his back. He'd picked up his meagre possession of tools from the barn, and walked down to the harbour.

There really wasn't much to repair. In truth he simply wanted to be alone and think, maybe figure out what he was going to do about Finn and Tom. At first when they'd singled him out for a bit of sport, he'd assumed it wouldn't last very long if he didn't engage with them. They seemed the type to grow bored and move onto another victim after a while. But they hadn't. If anything, it was getting worse.

He'd asked his father what to do. Of course, he was no help. "It's all part of becoming a man," he'd said.

His father, being the peaceful man he was, didn't give him any little gems of advice that would help his situation. There were no 'come on, Son. I'll teach you some moves, or 'I'll sort them out myself. No-one treats my Son that way'. He was on his own.

"I presume Finn and Tom had something to do with that fat lip?"

He turned to find Marissa standing on the pier, hands on hips, an eyebrow raised. Gren rolled his eyes at the Lord's daughter. "Top marks for stating the obvious, Rissa," he said sarcastically, resuming his boat maintenance.

She tilted her head to the side. "Now don't pout, Gren...actually, are you pouting? I can't tell with that thing attached to your face." She giggled, jumping into his boat, scattering his tools.

He smiled in spite of himself. Although annoying at times, Marissa always found a way to lift his mood. It was a rare gift. He also liked her complete disregard for social protocol. It was generally frowned upon for a high-born lady to mingle with commoners. She was either oblivious, or didn't care – he suspected it was the latter.

"Has the Lady of Daltons Hill not got any prior engagements to be tending to?" he asked in a mock tone, and bowing, knowing it irritated her.

She rolled her eyes at him. "So much you wouldn't believe, fisher-boy. But a Lady must make time for her loyal tenants." She waved a hand regally, and curtsied. Although said in jest, Gren knew Marissa actually felt she had a duty to spend time with her father's wards. It was another thing he admired about her – a sentiment held by most of the city. "If one is being bullied by trainees of the Lord's personal guard, it would be prudent to intervene."

His mood darkened a little at the mention of Finn and Tom. "I can handle the situation myself, Rissa."

She looked down at his lip, looking doubtful. "So, I see."

"So, what's been happening in Oakhaven? I heard you and your father were at the coronation," he asked, changing the subject.

She sat down next to him, her blonde curls bouncing about her shoulders. They smelled of lavender, he thought. He immediately shook the thought from his mind. "The place was a riot," she said. "The ceremony was low-key, of course, as befitting that lump of wood Skallen. Hal was a lot more fun." She frowned. "He was a good king. I feel for Queen Isabel. She was absent, recovering from her terrible injuries."

"Do they know who killed him?" he asked, regretting the way it came out. She raised an eyebrow at him. "You know what I mean," he said.

"Father attended a few meetings. He didn't say much to me about what was said. I asked him, but he told me to let the men deal with such matters," she said, a sadness crossing her features for a moment.

Marissa was Lord Cunningham's only child. Her mother had died during childbirth, giving birth to Marissa. It was common knowledge – but never spoken aloud – he resented her for not being the boy he wanted her to be. In Gren's mind, he was a fool. Marissa was smart, she respected her people, and they her. She also had a hardness to her befitting a good leader. He didn't think it mattered if a leader was a man or a woman, as long as they were good at ruling.

She continued. "From what I overheard from the serving staff, and a few noblemen who'd had a little too much claret, all fingers seem to be pointing towards Helven."

His eyes widened. If this proved true, war was almost a certainty. If there was ever a time to learn how to use a sword, it was now. A thought occurred to him. "What about the Knights of the Hour? Although rarely seen, and a bit scary and creepy when they are, shouldn't they get involved. According to the stories, this would fall under their remit as peacekeepers wouldn't it? Were any of their High Lords present for the coronation?"

Marissa leaned forward. "Their temple was destroyed. Supposedly, there's only one left, and he didn't leave Oakhaven on good terms with King Hal, shortly before his murder."

Gren's mouth hung open in shock. The Knights of the Hour were gone? They were legends. He used to love hearing the stories about them when he was younger – he still loved them if he was being honest. They couldn't be gone. The news was huge. Also worrying. What was happening to the world?

"When did this all happen?" he asked.

"About three weeks ago."

Gren looked towards the river. The direction of the current, and the place he'd found Lana meant she could only have come from one direction.

The direction of the temple.

~

Lana dropped down to the soft grass below her window without a sound. The night was quiet and peaceful. There was a cool breeze which she found comforting. She took in a deep lungful, and slowly exhaled feeling herself relax, almost as though she was becoming one with the night.

She took a stroll in the direction of the woods that lay beyond the farm's outer fence, the hem of her cloak brushing along the soft grass. She was maybe a quarter mile from the river on the other side of the woods. She could hear it faintly, along with the occasional sound of an owl out hunting its prey.

She vaulted the fence and looked back. Gren and his family were beginning to grow on her. They were kind people. As strange as it sounded, after all that had happened to her, she felt lucky Gren had found her. June had told her she could have been swept towards Oakhaven if she hadn't been washed up where she had.

She didn't know what to do next. She had nowhere to go. She felt certain once Gren's mother and father thought she was better, they would expect her to move on. It was a small cottage. They hadn't said, but she was sure they were struggling with an extra mouth to feed under their roof.

She sighed. She didn't want to leave, at least not yet. She wasn't ready. June had become very protective of her, fussing over her whenever she came downstairs, reminding her of her own mother. Stephen, Gren's father, didn't say much to her, though he didn't say much at all. But whenever he did, he was always kind in his words.

She liked Gren most of all. She didn't think he realised how much he brightened up a room whenever he was in it. He was clumsy, a dreamer, and had a unique humour which cheered her up whenever she was feeling down. She'd watched him playing in the yard with a stick, crudely fashioned in the shape of a sword. She suspected the life of a farmer wasn't very high on his list of priorities. This was an issue between him and Stephen, as Gren always waited until his father left for the market before he would practice with his stick and the block.

Watching his practice had amused her. He sorely needed a tutor. Anger filled her, as images of those two older boys bullying Gren sprang to mind. They needed bringing down a peg or two.

Thoughts for another day, she thought, as she turned from the cottage and ventured into the woods towards the river. She took her time traipsing through the trees, picking up wild flowers as she went. Eventually, she reached the river and sat down on a log which had washed up upon the bank.

She sat for a long time watching the river flow by, on its journey towards the sea. She spoke to her parents, telling them she loved and missed them as she laid the bunch of flowers onto the water. She watched as they were swept away by the current, disappearing into the gloom. She let her tears flow and drop between her boots.

Thoughts of her parents led to darker thoughts of the man in the black armour. The architect of her misery. Resolve began to take root in her. She couldn't stay hidden away, in fear of those who had murdered them. She would avenge them. Until her last breath she would look for a way to avenge them.

She was broken from her reverie by a deep growling behind her. She slowly turned, and found herself face to face with the biggest wolf she had ever seen. It slowly approached her from the copse, hunched low, its teeth bared in a snarl. The wolf's head was massive. She noticed the beast's fur appeared to be singed short on its left-hand side, which was odd.

Panic filled her. She was unarmed – though she didn't think her knife would be much use against the monstrosity currently approaching her.

It lifted its head and howled, curdling her blood. She frantically looked for an escape. The river posed the only viable option were getting ripped to shreds held the least. She stood up slowly, and began to back up towards the river.

To her horror, more wolves began to emerge from the woods. The fact they were smaller provided her with little solace. She backed up a little more, her boots splashing in the cold water – a reminder of her last exploits near it.

In her desperation, she picked up a small

rock, and held it aloft – for what little it would do against a pack of wolves. "Stay back," she shouted at them. She felt a heat filling her chest, similar to the sensation she'd felt when she had faced those dark men upon the cliff-top.

Then something strange happened.

They all dipped their heads, and took a step back. Now she was confused. What was happening? For a moment they stayed where they were. It was then she noticed the big wolf had stopped growling. It didn't even look angry anymore. It gave a gentle growl as it licked its muzzle.

"Let me past," she said. She didn't know why she said it, it just felt like the right thing to say.

To her shock and confusion, they complied, the pack splitting to create a path between them. Slowly she began to walk forward – all the while thinking she was going to get mauled at any second. Her heart hammered in her chest, threatening to burst through her ribcage, as she got further down the path of wolves. She was sure as she passed each wolf, in an almost debilitating state of terror, that more than a couple bowed their heads at her.

She didn't look back until she reached the edge of the woods, still convinced each step was going to be her last. She turned and faced them.

They were all staring at her. The anger she had felt, radiating off them like heat from a furnace, was now gone. The big one licked its muzzle once more and dipped its head at her. She decided now was not the time to spend internally debating the mental mysteries of a pack of wolves as they stood staring at her. Now was the time to tuck-tail and run.

She took a deep breath, turned, and ran as fast as her legs would take her. The sound of their howls growing more faint with each step.

Chapter Eleven - The Temple

A week since his audience with Cunningham, Kerr had left Daltons Hill and travelled through the Great Forest in a foul mood. His mind felt bogged down with the ever-growing number of questions he felt needed answering. He followed the ancient paths that would take him home, traversing around huge oaks, and close knitted rock formations that could've been remnants of villages from long ago for all he knew.

As he ventured deeper into the woods and away from civilisation, time felt different somehow, as though the hours and days seemed to stretch and linger that much longer. Or maybe it was because he spent the time running through everything that had happened to him since his flight from Oakhaven. It was hard to tell.

It was growing thicker too, he realised, as he began to travel through parts of the forest that saw less human traffic. Great vines and roots had begun to cover large parts of the path, as though the forest were attempting to claim it back. He'd lost count of the amount of times he'd had to dismount and hack at overgrown bushes and thickets to get his mare through – he'd pictured Cunningham's face on more than a few shrubs.

Thinking of that pompous ass gave him pause to think of all the changes that were happening within this realm in such a short time. With the possibility of his order being gone and a new king sitting on the throne with a less-than-pleasant opinion for his order, he wasn't sure what to do.

The life of a hermit was growing in appeal the more he dwelt on it.

After a few more days, he came across a small cottage, or what used to be a cottage, in the middle of a man-made clearing cut into the woods. Unlike the rock formations, which may have been homes to people many years ago, this ruin looked a lot fresher.

He'd come across it by chance as he'd been stalking a deer. His lapse in concentration had caused him to move a little too sudden and step on a dried piece of bark. With an audible crack he'd alerted his quarry to his presence and spooked it. He'd watched in frustration, as it fled with speed and agility in the opposite direction. It disappeared into the dark gloom of the forest.

Resigned to more dried meat from his pack, he'd pushed his way through the foliage and into the clearing.

He stood and stared at the pile of rubble that used to be someone's home. It was quiet. He didn't like it. He unclipped his hammer, the motion automatic, and rested it on his shoulder. If there was anyone lying in wait to spring an ambush, he would be ready.

Taking his time, he began to circle the ruin. He observed every detail as he made his way around the outer edges of the clearing. Once he'd completed a full circuit, and found nothing to suggest he wasn't the only one in the vicinity, he clipped his hammer onto his back.

He nodded to himself and slowly approached the ruin for a closer inspection.

To one side of the rubble, lay two freshly dug graves; the soil still dark and moist. What confused him slightly, were the two bodies lying next to the graves. He was thankful for the gentle breeze, as the aroma of rotting flesh was lighter than it could have been. He rubbed a calloused hand over his chin, his fingers scratching at the beginnings of a beard, trying to picture the scene that had played out. They'd hardly filled the two holes and then dropped down dead.

The two corpses looked to be soldiers of some kind – he didn't recognise the strange black armour they donned. The way their bodies were splayed out unnaturally, and the wounds inflicted upon them, suggested they'd died by furious violence.

The clearing had been attacked, that much was obvious to him. He presumed the ruined cottages inhabitants were now residing in the two freshly dug plots. It looked like they had been killed by the dead soldiers lying in front of him. The soldiers had been surprised and slain themselves sometime after.

His gaze settled on the ruin once more. He shook his head. He was still missing something. How had only two soldiers reduced a cottage to a pile of broken masonry? Who had killed them? Who were the two buried in the graves? The two may have been left behind to sentry, possibly because their group suspected there would be others that either stayed or visited the clearing.

If so, they had been correct.

One thing he did know, the person – or people – who'd killed the soldiers had cared for the two in the graves. Flowers had been lain on each mound, arranged in an intricate design which could only have come from a place of deep love and sorrow. A great deal of time had been spent crafting it. Its design was beautiful, strangely he found something familiar about it.

He took a step back and scrutinised the pattern, following its many colours, and directions as it took its shape trying to think where he'd recognised it from. Then it dawned on him. He slowly raised a hand to his open mouth as he recognised the pattern the flowers made. It was a pattern he'd been around his entire life. How had he missed it?

It was the sigil of the Hour. His sigil.

Was it possible a Knight of the Hour had done this? He began to doubt the idea of him being the last of his order, just as Judiah had suggested with his cryptic prophesies. In the back of his mind he hoped he was right. Maybe they were back at the temple.

Another thought occurred to him. Was he standing over the graves of two Knights of the Hour? It was entirely possible. If so, why did they not reside at the temple as was their custom? He grew hopeful, but it was mingled with frustration. The closer he got to the temple, the stranger things seemed to get.

He looked up at the evening sky; the clouds tinged with pink. There wasn't much sunlight left, and he felt weary. Deciding the clearing was as good a place as any to set up camp, he hurried back to where he'd left the horse, and hoped to find some answers soon.

~

He woke in front of the cottage feeling as though he'd slept for minutes rather than hours. His sleep had been plagued with dreams of fire and destruction. Of men in black armour, their faces deathly white, surrounding him amidst the darkness.

He sat up and rubbed his eyes. His stomach rumbled its complaint. He looked over at his pack ruefully. The thought of more dried meat spurred him to get up and venture into the woods in search of something better to eat for breakfast.

After an hour of patient hunting, he managed to bag a couple of rabbits which he made into a stew with some herbs. He sat contentedly, eating the rich broth – savouring the moist meat as it slipped down his throat, before setting off through the forest towards home.

The next few days passed with a strange

sort of repetition. Eating up as many miles as possible before it got too dark to continue on without getting lost, setting up camp, and enduring more troubled sleep.

Eventually he reached a familiar sight as the trees began to thin out. The watchtower sat on a hill overlooking the forest for many miles. It was ringed with a parapet with gaps in-between for archers to fire from. He climbed the hill towards it knowing he would find out if Skallen's reports were true when he reached the top.

As he got closer, he knew he wouldn't need to reach the top of the hill to know the fate of his brethren. Half the parapet was missing, as though it had been struck with a rock or boulder the size of a house. A body hung from one of the gaps, broken by whatever had crashed into the tower. Dried blood streaked the brickwork underneath the body. He kicked the horse's flanks, sending her into a gallop to the top of the hill.

What he saw when he reached the top took his breath away. He sat in the saddle open mouthed. There was nothing left. The temple grounds were in complete ruin, as though a great battle had ripped through it. Most of the buildings were either in a state of complete collapse or on the verge of. The temple's domed roof at the centre had collapsed in on itself.

He was half a mile away, but he could still make out the bodies strewn everywhere. He kicked the horse's side once more, and flew towards the main entrance.

He had to slow his mare the last hundred yards, as the road leading into the temple grounds were littered with the dead. He took in every body as he drew closer to the arch, their faces in various expressions of surprise and horror. The place reeked of death and shit. He raised a hand to his nose, releasing a little of his power to block his nasal receptors. He felt himself retch as he passed a boy, no more than ten, having been struck down from an arrow to the back; his face slack-jawed, his eyes gone, picked clean by the scavengers that circled above his head.

He dismounted under the arch and continued on towards the temple itself, leaving his horse behind to feed on the grass by the side of the road.

He passed houses and workshops, stables and meeting halls, in ruin. Some had been burned from the inside out. Others looked as though they had been destroyed by something more devastating than fire. These were structures he had spent his childhood around. Some of the homes he passed belonged to friends and colleagues. He was finding it difficult to process his emotions on the sights before him.

He didn't know where to begin.

He eventually reached the central courtyard. At its centre lay the temple of the Hour. Some of the roof had spilled out through the entrance at the top of the stone steps leading up to it. He called out to see if there was anyone inside, his voice echoing, though he knew he'd receive no answer to his calls.

He sank to his knees, the last Knight of the Hour, and wept for a time. His tears littered the dusty ground. His sobs reverberating around the broken masonry.

When he felt he could not weep anymore, he slowly climbed back to his feet and climbed the steps up to the temple, feeling weak and tired. When he reached the top, he found the entrance was blocked by one of the stone pillars which had collapsed.

His remaining energy felt spent, so he decided to sit on a piece of roof by the main doors. He gazed back towards the way he'd came and began trying to process the destruction around him. It looked as though there was barely any resistance. Maybe Skallen's intelligence had been correct. Maybe the Hour had been infiltrated from within. He looked down at a dead Cleric, lying at an odd angle in front of a set of stables to his right. He'd never know. The thought of not knowing set his teeth on edge.

He sighed, deciding to fetch his horse and find something to eat. As he rose, a hand touched his shoulder. Instinct took over. He whirled round and grabbed whoever had surprised him by the throat. The face of a gaunt looking woman looked back at him, her face growing purple as he choked her. Her eyes were wild, tears streaming down them. She began to struggle and slap at his wrists.

Recognition dawned on him as he knew the face.

Rian.

He let go immediately. Rian dropped to the stone floor coughing and spluttering.

"Rian," he shouted. "Rian, you're alive. How is that possible?"

She rubbed her throat and glared up at him. She looked as though she was about to throw a volley of insults in his direction, but instead opted to break down in tears. Kerr knelt down and hugged her – she was so thin, he thought. They remained where they were for a time, holding one another, their grief filling the empty ruins of their broken home.

He pulled his head back and took hers between his hands. She was cold, she looked so gaunt in stark contrast to the wild, rosy cheeked loud-mouthed Cleric he had grown up with. "Rian, where are the others? The Knights? The Clerics?" Her beautiful brown eyes stared back at him, full of loss and despair. She shook her head. "The High Lords?" he asked.

She placed her hands over his own, still resting on her cheeks, holding them in her own, and looked down. "They were in the temple when it caved in on itself. There was so much fire and destruction, Kerr. I can still hear their screams and shouts inside my head."

He opened his mouth to ask another

question, then decided against it for the moment. "I'll head back into the forest and fetch us something to eat." He rose, and turned towards the steps.

She shot an arm out, gripping his sleeve. "Don't leave me alone, Kerr. Please. I can't stand the silence anymore." She gave him an expression that seemed feral – which he understood, given what horrors she had witnessed.

He gently pulled her to her feet. "Never," he said. Her shoulders relaxed at his reassurance. "Come. We'll go together."

With their arms around each other, they slowly headed towards the forest in search of food.

Chapter Twelve – Grace

From the solitude and darkness of the rooftop, the hooded man watched the procession below him. King Hal's huge coffin, carried within a golden carriage, and pulled by two massive war horses, made its slow journey towards the holy hall and his final resting place. The carriage was flanked on either side by holy men; dressed in white, their cowl's hiding their faces from view as they each held torches which bathed the procession in a warm orange glow. He surmised the intention was to show both the faith and the crown were beacons of light in the darkness. A sign to the citizens who had turned up in droves.

He'd never met the man, but from the turn out below it was more than obvious the king was loved. More than a few were weeping openly.

The new King, Skallen, followed in the carriage's wake. His head was bowed in reverence to his older brother. He noted the Queen was absent. He'd heard she was in the palace, still recovering from her ordeal. It saddened him. A spouse should be present when their partner was laid to rest. To say a final goodbye. It made him think of his two friends back at the clearing. Buried together, their passing similar to King Hal's.

He thought of the girl. He'd followed the path of the river towards Oakhaven. He'd taken his time searching the riverbanks for signs of her. He'd assumed she'd known where the river lead, and somehow managed to drift to the capital, perhaps by grabbing onto a piece of driftwood. He had his doubts but it was all he had to go on.

When he'd reached Oakhaven, news of the King's murder had been the talk of the city. He'd been shocked when he'd heard. Most shocking of all was news of a Knight of the Hour falling out with King Hal, assaulting his guards, and fleeing the city around the time of his death. After a little digging, he'd found where the knight had been staying.

A room at an inn within the poorer area of the city. The inn who's roof he was currently standing on.

He waited until the procession disappeared from view, taking most of the crowd with it, and climbed down, dropping into an alley. A side door the inn must have used to take deliveries lay slightly ajar. He slowly opened it, making sure there was no-one behind it, and slipped inside.

He crept down a narrow corridor, passing an empty room that looked to be a staffroom of some sort, which was empty. He could hear a cacophony of voices at the far end of the corridor, presumably from the bar. Like a ghost he quickly tip-toed to the end of the corridor and entered the room unnoticed, taking a seat at the bar.

It was fairly busy. There were maybe

twenty people, either sitting in the booths that lined the back wall, or standing at the bar. Behind the bar, stood a tall, skinny man, with a large hooked nose. He was filling wooden mugs and placing them on trays. He looked to be the innkeeper. He caught the innkeeper's eye as he glanced over in his direction. The innkeeper's eyes widened in fear as he dropped one of the mugs onto the floor, spilling the contents over his shoes.

A few of the locals followed the innkeepers gaze. One pointed at him. "Is that the guy you mentioned, Banks?"

If there was any doubt the knight had resided at the inn, it had now vanished. He was in the right place alright. The knight must have made a similar exit from here as he did the palace.

He thought he'd lend a hand before the situation grew ugly. He removed his hood. The innkeeper sighed in what looked like relief.

"No, it's not him, Gus," he said, approaching him. "You a knight as well? We were told he was the last of them. The rest all killed up at the temple." Although he seemed relieved he was not his previous tenant, he still eyed the hooded man with suspicion. The hooded man felt his guts tighten at the mention of the temple. The innkeeper faced him, resting his elbows on the bar-top. His breath smelled of garlic and stale ale. "Didn't even know he was one of them. Thought he was a mercenary, or a hedge knight. Made quite an exit. Beat up four men from the guild, damn near wrecked one of my rooms."

The hooded man didn't like the look of this fellow. Maybe it was the way his eyes flitted about, as though in search of where his coin was most likely situated on his person. He threw him a smile, he was here to find answers, not enemies. "I'm no Knight of the Hour, friend. Just a simple traveller come to pay my respects to the King," he said, making a sign in the air with his hand.

The innkeeper nodded, making the same sign himself. He nodded down at his robes, his brow furrowing. "I must say though, you are dressed awfully similar. What's with the robes?"

"It's cold and this keeps me warm," he said, shrugging.

The innkeeper snorted, a horrible nasally sound that irritated his ears. "Well I'd consider wearing something else, traveller. Not a popular thing to be wearing in these parts. That knight caused a lot of trouble when he left the city. The King's men want him for questioning, the guild compensated for the slight."

"What sort of questions?" he asked.

The innkeeper leant closer, his rancid breath crawling up his nostrils almost making him recoil. "His whereabouts around the time of good King Hal's passing. He left my inn a few days before it happened. If you ask me, I think that whore-son held back and killed the King before leaving."

The hooded man raised his eyebrows. "Is that so?"

The innkeeper shrugged. "Wouldn't put it past him. I don't mind telling you, friend, he was an odd sort that one. Very unsavoury character."

The hooded man nodded, thinking it took one to know one. He didn't like this innkeeper at all.

The innkeeper continued. "I'm Banks by the way. Ale? Bed and board?"

His first instinct was to decline this horrible little man, but it was late and he'd no energy to venture out into the streets in search of another inn. He nodded, to which Banks slammed a hand on the bar. "Excellent, a wise choice. Best inn this quarter of the city." he raised his hand, pointing over to one of the tables behind him. "Take a seat and I'll get the girl to bring you some ale." He leaned forward once more. "She can serve in other ways if you catch my drift. Just say the word."

Before he'd succumbed to the urge of slamming Banks' face on the bar, the innkeeper turned. He shouted to a pretty barmaid tending to one of the patrons seated at a table on the other side of the room. "Grace, bring a mug of ale to our traveller friend. See that he's made to feel welcome."

The barmaid gave Banks a sheepish nod, and walked behind the bar to fill a flagon. The hooded man turned away from Banks and took a seat at a table.

The barmaid approached with a mug full of frothy ale. Her blonde curly hair was parted so that it covered one side of her face. She put the mug down in front of him and smiled. It was then he noticed her hair had been parted to hide a nasty looking bruise under her eye. She looked miserable. He noticed she was staring at his robes. She looked away when she caught his eye.

He gestured to the empty chair opposite him. She nodded and sat down. "Do you need anything else besides the ale, Sir?" she asked. A vacant look crossed her features as she slowly run a hand down her chest. He suspected it was to entice him to consider a more private service. To the hooded man, it just looked wrong.

He reached over and took her hand. She flinched slightly, but didn't pull her hand from under his. "The ale is fine, my dear. If you would stay and keep me company, that is all I ask."

She relaxed a little. She looked him in the eyes. "You look like him, you know."

"Like who?"

She slowly turned her head towards the bar, then back, as though to make sure she wasn't being eavesdropped. "Like Lord Kerr."

It didn't take a genius to know who she was referring to. "The Knight?"

She nodded. "He's a good man. He was always nice to me. It's not true what they're all saying about him."

"Who have been saying what about him?"

She pulled her hand from under his. "Nothing. It doesn't matter." She got up to leave. "If that'll be all, I need to see if any of the other customers need tending to."

The girl was clearly terrified. He suspected Banks had a lot to do with it. He raised a hand and smiled. "It's okay, Grace." He gestured to her chair. "Please, sit down. Tell me of this knight."

She paused for a moment, as though fighting an internal struggle. She eventually relented and took her seat once more. "You're not from the palace, are you?"

He laughed. She narrowed her eyes at him, not sharing his amusement. "Do I look like a palace spy?" he asked.

She looked him up and down. "I suppose not." She smiled, dimples forming at on her cheeks.

"What has been said about the knight?" he asked.

"They say he's responsible for the death of King Hal. But they're all wrong," she whispered.

He took another sip of ale. "What made him leave the city? Some would call that suspicious, wouldn't you agree."

She shook her head emphatically. "He had to leave. His home had been destroyed. We didn't know it at the time as we didn't know he was a Knight of the Hour. When I first met him, I thought he was a nobleman, as he seemed more refined than the rest of our clientele. But he was a Knight, from the temple. That's supposedly what his argument with the King was about. He came back here and four guild thugs were waiting for him in his room. I warned him before they could surprise him." She sighed, exasperated. "I was so angry with him for leaving. I just didn't know."

The hooded man was beginning to suspect all was not what it seemed. It was a bit of a coincidence there had been men waiting for the knight after he'd gotten back from his disastrous meeting with the King. Then he'd been killed a few days later.

The hooded man closed his eyes, rubbing his temples. With the King dead, the temple destroyed, his friends killed and their daughter missing, all in such a small space of time. It felt more than just coincidence. And now this knight – the last knight – possibly being accused of regicide. It felt as though they were pieces on a chess board being manoeuvred into place for something. But for what, he didn't know.

Grace was staring at him. Her hair had parted revealing the bruise.

"Did Banks give you that?" he asked, nodding at her black eye.

She gasped, a look of fear marring her features. "The innkeeper put two and two together and figured out I'd told Lord Kerr about the men in his room. I only used to serve drinks. After what happened, he said he owed the guild a lot of money for what happened to their men. He said that was my debt, and I wasn't going to clear it by serving drinks." Her eyes became glassy. "He makes me do things... for the customers. For him."

She looked like she was about to vomit. The hooded man glanced over towards where Banks was seated, laughing at a joke one of his customers was telling him. Anger began to well in him, like a pyre that had just caught a spark and erupted into life.

Grace caught the look and grabbed his arm. "Please don't say anything to him. I've got nowhere else to go."

He put a hand on her arm. "You won't need to go anywhere." He smiled, and rose from his seat. "Wait here, I'll be back in a minute."

Before she could reply, he walked passed her and approached the bar. Banks smiled at him, causing the urge to strike him all the more tempting. "Is everything alright?" he asked, casting an irritated glance towards Grace. "Not causing you grief, is she? She's a bit stupid, sometimes needs brought to heel." A vile, leering smile spread across his face as he raised his hands up to his chest. "But she makes up for it in other ways," he said, winking at him.

"That's what I've come over to speak to you about," he said, cutting the repulsive innkeeper off before he went on any further. "The girl has been a delight, exactly what this weary traveller has been in need of. I'd like to obtain her services for the rest of the night. I can pay," he said, pulling out a bag of coins from within his cloak.

A greedy gleam passed over Banks' face. He made a pathetic show of switching his expression to one of business, as though the prostitution of one of his barmaids were the same as if they were bartering over the price of his drinks. The man was a worm. "Although I said she's a bit thick between the ears, that don't mean her services are cheap. I'll take five gold for the night."

The hooded man nodded and dropped ten gold coins on the bar, eliciting more than a few of Banks' regulars to glance over with interest. "Take ten. I'll expect a meal and a jug of ale for the both of us."

Banks began to nod like an idiot as he scooped the coins and dropped them into the pouch on his apron. He handed him a key from under the bar. "Your food will be brought up to your room shortly, friend. Enjoy the girl."

The hooded man forced a smile and turned back towards his table, feeling the urge to have a bath after spending too much time in that horrible little man's presence for too long.

He sat down opposite Grace and smiled. "I've got you for the night," he said, then regretted the way the words came out the second they left his lips.

Her expression was one of betrayal. "I thought you didn't want me to do that? That all you wanted to do was talk?"

Despite her look of panic, he couldn't help but chuckle. He waved a hand at her, shaking his head. "Grace, I've ordered some food and ale for the room I've just rented from your employer. We're going to go up, have a bite to eat, drink a few mugs of good ale, then you're going to rest. You look miserable and exhausted."

She raised the eyebrow that wasn't cover with her hair. "And where are you going to sleep?"

"I'm not. I'm going to slip out the window. I'll be out most of the night, I have some business to take care of."

Despite his reassurances she still remained sceptical. "Why would you do that? I don't even know you."

He leaned forward. "Because this world is going to shit, and there are too many bullies taking advantage of good people."

~

Banks closed the door as the last of the drunks left the inn and staggered out into the night. He locked the door and strolled behind the bar. He poured himself an ale, and began to count the night's takings. It had been a very profitable night, he thought, pleased.

He looked up towards the ceiling. Grace would be entertaining her guest, the thought of her curvy little body bouncing up and down sent a stirring in his loins. Ten gold. He chuckled to himself. She was good, not ten gold good though.

The little cow was slowly making up for her betrayal. And after he'd taken her in when she had nowhere else to go. Put a roof over her head, and decent coin in her ungrateful hand. How had she paid him in return? By giving the heads up to that traitor knight, which ended in a perfectly good room being wrecked and three guildsmen beaten and broken on his floorboards – well, it was really two as one of them had been thrown out the window. He'd had to compensate the guild for the embarrassment. At a heavy price.

He allowed himself a smile. She was paying the price now. After he'd figured out it was her, he'd lain down the new rules for her employment. She'd protested at first, but he'd threatened to tell the guild about her involvement and she'd quickly acquiesced.

He'd sampled her first, of course. Beaten her a little into the bargain. The thought of her lying underneath him, squirming, was one of sheer ecstasy. He'd only lasted a few minutes, but it was enjoyable all the same.

He hadn't liked the look of that vagrant traveller. But business was business. He'd certainly liked the fool's coin. He finished his ale and poured himself another. He drank greedily, relishing the frothy beer as it slipped down his throat. He had to admit, he did make a fine ale.

Suddenly a thump, coming from the back, broke him from his reverie. "Grace?" he called. "That you?" He received no reply. Must be the ale, he thought.

Then he heard it again. Louder this time. He slammed his mug down and stormed towards it. If that idiot girl was back there causing a raucous there'd be hell to pay.

He bashed the door open with the palm of his hand to find it empty. The room was dark and gloomy. He shook his head. Maybe he'd had more ale than he'd thought.

He was about to turn when something tapped him on the shoulder. Instinctively, he whirled around to face whoever was behind him. Something hard struck his nose. A blinding whiteness flashed before his eyes as he heard the audible crunch of his nose breaking. He felt warm blood flow down over his mouth, running freely from his chin to the floor below.

He stumbled back, groaning in pain, holding his ruined nose. His assailant didn't let up though. With speed he'd never witnessed, he was dealt a flurry of kicks and punches all over his body. He felt ribs crack, and teeth fly out of his mouth. His kneecap was kicked out of place, sending him to the floor. He tried to scream or yelp in pain, his attacker was too fast to let him.

His assailant paused for a few seconds as Banks lay on the floor, praying his assailant was done with him. He was wrong. He felt a hand roughly grab a hank of his hair and pull him to his feet. His knee felt as though a white-hot knife had been left in there to torment him. All thoughts and sense momentarily left him as his face was smashed repeatedly against the breakfast table. He felt his bladder give up on him as warm piss and shit ran down his legs.

Then as fast as the onslaught had started, it finished as he was dropped to the ground.

His vision swam. His whole body felt as though it were on fire. He was vaguely aware of a whining noise he suspected was coming from himself.

He felt a hand grab his face and pull it round. A shadow hovered over him. "This is what's going to happen. You're going to pack up your shit. You're going to sign that document I've left on the table. The deeds of this inn will pass to the barmaid you have been abusing."

Banks began to protest in the form of blood-spattered incoherent babbling as his teeth had shredded his lips during the assault. Leave his bar to that little whore. The business he built from the ground up. The hell he would.

His assailant must have been able to read his expression – which he found oddly impressive as he surmised his face must have looked like something that would look quite at home on a butcher's block. Through his broken vision, he could only make out the silhouette of a head shaking in disappointment.

With lightning speed, his assailant grabbed his hand and separated the index finger from the rest, and in one quick motion snapped it back. Banks gave a high-pitched squeal as he felt the bone break, piercing through the skin. The man then proceeded to break the rest of the fingers on his left hand as he bucked and writhed, filling the room with the sounds of complete and utter agony.

He was let go once more to roll and cry on the floor. The man grabbed his ruined face once more and began to whisper in his ear. "I do hope you write with your right hand. Now let me continue, you will leave the bar to Grace, pack your belongings, and leave the city."

"But the guild. They won't like it. They'll kill me. I owe them one hundred gold for their men. For what that knight done."

The man slapped him. "The guild won't cause any problems. They've been paid. Though you don't deserve it, I've left you some gold to be on your way. Do this and you'll never see me again. If not? I'll leave that to your imagination. The human body has quite a lot of bones."

Banks lay there, waiting for a further beating. It never came. He looked up to find he was the only one in the room.

With some effort, he managed to drag himself over to the table and pull his broken body onto the seat. The man had been right. On the table sat a deed transfer, a quill, and an inkwell.

At first, he'd thought his attacker was the traveller who had purchased Grace. But this man seemed bigger. Besides, the traveller looked too old to be able to administer that amount of furious violence. He was at a loss. His mind felt too scrambled. He looked down at the document. Its header read 'Property transfer'.

With tears running down his face, broken and humiliated, he picked up the quill.

~

From the shadows of the alley outside, the hooded man took one last look up at the window of the room Grace was currently sleeping in. He'd dropped a sleeping tonic in her ale so she wouldn't be woken by the noise downstairs. She would wake feeling refreshed from such a deep sleep.

He felt good. He was certain it would go as planned. After she'd fallen asleep, he put her to bed, slipped out, and made a few arrangements. The guild would receive their payment via the crown bank with the stipulation it would be paid the minute a deed transfer in Grace's name – as the inn's new owner – went through. If Banks didn't sign it, he'd have the guild to deal with. He would see that when he read the document.

Smiling at the image of Grace coming across the deed transfer in the morning, the hooded man walked down the alley, disappearing into the night.

Chapter Thirteen - A Fight Amongst the Ruins

They spent the next few days clearing the roads of debris, piling the bodies up on a pyre they'd constructed in front of the temple. It was physically and emotionally exhausting. Kerr had to stop more than once, usually after laying one of the children down. He'd kneel down with the body in front of him, and say a silent prayer through tears that rolled freely down his cheeks, the promise of retribution burning stronger with each body he prepared, forever on his mind.

He reminded himself it was better this way, their bodies commemorated on a pyre, to aid in their spirits journey to the halls of their fathers. Better that than their rotting corpses left out in the sun, to be picked clean by the carrion birds that seemed to hover above their heads like a macabre cloud.

He spoke to Rian as they worked. It was mostly small talk to help take their minds off what they were doing, and the severity of their situation, helping to sooth their ragged grief. She gave him one-word answers to begin with, but eventually began to come out of her shell, opening up a little more each day. He felt he had to be patient with her, despite how desperate he was for information.

He laid down the body of a stable-boy he'd known, and turned to Rian who'd given up on the dead for the day, her eyes red-rimmed and puffy. Instead, she chose to move some of the boulders and rocks, though her body language told him she wasn't fully committed to the task. Her hair was plastered to her face, her features screwed up as she worked. She looked as bad as he felt.

"Rian," he called over to her. She looked his way, holding a hand up to shield her eyes from the glare of the noon sun. "I'm going to fetch us something to eat. Will you be alright here for a short while? I won't be long."

She nodded, then resumed her half-hearted attempt at moving the broken masonry.

He picked up a bow and quiver he'd found in one of the houses the day before, and trudged through some hedges into the woods.

~

Kerr kept low, choosing each step carefully as he slowly crept closer to a decent sized doe, about fifty yards in front of him. She had her back to him – though he knew that wasn't an excuse to grow complacent, his memory flitting back to the deer he'd spooked at the clearing. The deer's hearing was so attuned to the slightest noise, it really didn't matter which way it was facing.

Satisfied he was in a decent position, he raised the bow, and drew back the string, the end of the arrow nestled tightly between his fore and middle fingers. He began to feel a slow burn creep up the muscles on his arm, and down his back. He closed an eye and waited for the deer to raise her head.

He didn't have to wait long. The deer raised its head, and turned in his direction. No doubt she saw him standing there. Before he gave her a chance to react, he let the arrow go. He watched as it soared towards her, striking true as she began to buck in surprise, eventually stumbling, then falling to the ground.

He ran over to her and drew his knife. The deer was still trying to get up as he knelt down beside it, its limbs kicking in all directions. He ignored the wetness to his knees as the deer's blood seeped through the thin cloth, warm to his skin. He glanced at the shot he'd made. It was good, the arrow had almost passed straight through. He must have nicked an artery as there was already quite a lot of blood soaking the forest floor. He pulled its head back and drew the blade across its throat, finishing it so as not to prolong the poor beast's suffering.

He wiped the knife on the carcass and stood up, sighing with relief. This would help bring back both their strength. He looked back towards the direction of the temple. He could just make out the top of the dome – or what was left of it. They would eat some good fresh meat, then they would have a talk.

It was time.

With one heft, he lifted the deer up onto his shoulders, and slowly marched towards camp.

~

Kerr spent the rest of the afternoon, preparing the meat, while Rian foraged for berries, and fruit. She filled two pails of water – one for drinking, the other for washing.

They sat, enjoying each other's company, while the meat cooked on the fire. Surprisingly, it was Rian who broke the silence.

"Go on then, ask," she said.

Kerr raised his eyebrows. "Ask what?" he said.

She narrowed her eyes at him. "You know what." She raised a hand, gesturing around at the wreckage. "You want to know what happened. I appreciate you giving me a few days. It's been hard. To be honest, I don't know what I would've done if you hadn't shown up." She paused, looking down at her feet, a dark expression crossed her features. He could see tears begin to form in the corners of her eyes. She looked back up at him and smiled. "But I'm glad that you did."

He gave her a smile in return, though it didn't reach his eyes. "I don't really know where to start, Rian," he said, rubbing his temples. "I've travelled a long way to get here. A thousand questions have passed through my mind. Now that I'm here, and seen first-hand the devastation, most of those questions don't matter anymore." He paused a moment. "How did this happen?"

Rian remained silent for a moment, from her expression he didn't think he would get the answer he sought. "I don't know, Kerr. I really don't. The day it happened, everything was fine. I was with Joren, in the Alchemy workshop, when I heard the first of the screaming."

She began to rub her hands together; a faraway look crossed her face as though she were reliving the memory. Kerr remained quiet, letting her get it out in her own time.

She shook her head and continued. "We both ran outside to see what all the commotion was about. It was crazy. There was a bluish, blackish fog everywhere. We could barely see our hands in front of our faces. Every now and then, we would see a white flash, usually followed by a shout or a scream. It was hard to find our bearings. Eventually I lost Joren in the panic." She wiped a tear from her cheek. "I found him later on. Something had blasted a hole in his chest." She looked him in the eye, the tears falling freely. "He was my uncle, Kerr, my uncle."

Kerr nodded. He'd known Joren. A quiet little man who loved nothing more than pouring over powders and potions in his dark dusty laboratory. "What was the black smoke, Rian? Where did it come from? What about the High Lords, the Knights, the other Clerics?"

She shook her head emphatically. "I don't know. Not long after the screaming had started, the sounds of buildings being ripped apart started to fill my ears. I tried to make my way towards the temple. It was hard, I could barely see. I had to step over more and more of our dead. The children, Kerr. They even killed the children. I can still see their broken little faces looking up at me. There was nothing I could do for them. I'm a Cleric. I'm supposed to be a healer, and I couldn't save them."

She had begun to shake. Kerr got up, and sat down beside her. He put an arm around her shoulders.

"There was nothing you could do to save them, Rian. They were already gone. It's not your fault. We can speak about it another night," he said.

She waved a hand dismissively. "It's alright. If I don't let it all out now, there's a good chance I never will. I got as far as the courtyard in front of the temple when it collapsed. That was when it happened."

"When what happened?"

"The light. From within the temple. It came from inside the wreckage. It spilled out through every crack and gap. There were screams from inside. Then it went quiet."

"What happened to you, Rian? How were

you the only one to survive?" It was a question that had bothered him since they'd been reunited.

She shrugged. "I don't know. I tried to move some of the masonry to get into the temple, but it was no use, so I turned and ran towards the woods. I didn't get far though. A house blew apart next to me. I felt myself being thrown through the air, then it went black. I woke to find everyone gone, everything destroyed."

Kerr held her as she quietly sobbed. He could feel tears of his own prickling his cheeks. He'd thought he'd finally find the answers he'd been looking for when he arrived. But now he felt he was no closer to the truth than he'd been in Oakhaven when Skallen announced the temple's destruction. He got up and began to pace in front of the fire.

Rian watched him in silence as he walked back and forth. He didn't know where to go from here, asides from return to the capital. It hardly filled him with enthusiasm, but what else was there? He stopped and faced Rian. "What do we do now?" he asked.

She didn't reply. Her eyes were as wide as saucers. She pointed behind him. "Kerr, look out..."

He barely had time to register her words, before an arrow struck him in the shoulder.

Kerr staggered back and fell to his knees, his shoulder ablaze with pain. He didn't have time to deal with it though. Instinctively he rolled to the side, taking cover behind a large piece of masonry. He shouted to Rian, for her to run for cover. She shot up, and ran between a crumbled building, disappearing from view.

He could hear several voices, but they were incoherent. The pain in his shoulder voiced a complaint. He looked down at the wound. It wasn't deep, though that didn't stop it from hurting like a bastard. He grabbed the arrow, wincing as a lance of pain shot down his arm, mixed with a feeling of nausea causing his vision to swim for a second. Hoping the arrow tip wasn't barbed, he pulled it out, relieved to find it wasn't. Lucky the archer was a lousy shot, he thought, otherwise he'd be dead.

He quickly surveyed his surroundings. He needed an escape plan. Crouched in his current position, he was a sitting duck. It would only be a matter of time before they found him – whoever they were. It wouldn't take his assailants long to figure it out either.

He poked his head around the boulder, in search of anything resembling sanctuary. He spotted a gap that lead into the woods at the edge of their camp. The only problem was it was thirty feet from his current position. If he ran, the archer would surely spot him, spitting him like a prize pig. But there didn't seem to be any other options, he thought grimly. He didn't know how many of them there were, and where they were. It was the only way. He had to try.

What he needed, was something to distract the archer, if only for a couple of seconds. Luckily, the place was full of what he needed – an abundance of debris. He picked up a large rock – finding the weight of it in his hand oddly comforting.

He took a few quick breaths and launched himself out from cover, throwing the rock at the archer, aiming for his head. The archer spotted him, but was unable to get a shot off as he caught sight of the rock hurtling towards him. The archer dropped to a crouch as the rock flew over his head. Kerr felt a wave of disappointment that he'd chosen to duck. The distraction gave Kerr all the time he needed to close the distance to the gap without getting spit with another arrow.

Relying on blind faith, he leapt through the gap. He found, much to his chagrin, the terrain dipped, leading down a steep hill. He rolled and tumbled, his shoulder complaining the entire time, as he felt rocks, and roots tear at his clothing and skin. He landed with a thump at the bottom, feeling as though he'd just lost a fight with a mountain lion.

He heard voices grow closer to the top of the hill as he pulled himself to his feet. Fortunately, he'd landed on the path that ran around the temple grounds. He turned to the left and ran along the path that lead to the main road. At the moment, his only advantage was that he knew the grounds better than they did.

He raced along the path, adrenaline coursed through his veins, relegating the pain to the back of his mind. For now, he didn't have time for pain. Only survival. He only hoped Rian had found somewhere to hide.

He reached the line of bushes that flanked the road which approached the main arch. Keeping low, he quickly followed its path towards the it.

The line of bushes stopped short of the main entrance – about twenty feet. Peering over the top, he saw a soldier standing under the arch. He pulled his throwing dagger from its sheath, and summoned his energy into it. It began to glow faintly. He pushed through the foliage, and without pausing, threw the dagger at the sentry. It flew with lightning speed, connecting with the soldier's eye, and passing out the back of his head, spraying the rocks behind him with blood and brain matter.

The soldier staggered back, a look of shock and horror etched upon his ruined face. Blood soon covered his features, gushing out from the wound in great spurts, as he fell to the ground. Kerr approached the soldier and relieved him of his sword – he didn't need it anymore, being dead and all.

Switching from cover to cover, he slowly made his way back to camp. When he reached it, it was empty. He was relieved to find his pack was still where he'd left it. His hammer was there too, though it looked as though one of the soldiers had tried to move it, then gave up. Rian was nowhere to be seen either.

The sound of voices growing closer broke him from his reverie. He clipped the hammer onto his back and took cover. Three soldiers came into view; two were carrying short swords, followed by the archer at the rear. They proceeded with caution as they approached the camp, trading a few whispered words to each other as they went.

Very slowly, keeping low amongst the rocks and boulders, Kerr circled around the outside of the camp, flanking them.

He stopped when there was a break in the masonry too large to pass without being spotted. He crouched where he was and remained hidden, patiently waiting for an opportunity.

The soldiers reached his pack. One of them picked it up and said something to his comrade. He couldn't hear what was said, but he pointed past the camp, probably assuming he'd ventured further into the temple grounds to evade capture. He smiled to himself.

After they'd made a few more steps, Kerr broke cover and followed the soldiers. He was roughly ten yards behind the archer, when the soldier who'd picked up his pack turned and spotted him.

He pointed at Kerr, "Behind you, Galt," he shouted.

It was too late for Galt. Kerr took two

quick strides and swung the sword at Galt's neck with all the strength he could muster. The sword cut three quarters of the way into his neck. Kerr let go of the sword, and unclipped his hammer.

The two soldiers watched in ashen faced horror as their friend's head swung over like a trap door, the sword clattering to the ground, as an eruption of blood spewed from the gaping maw his neck had become.

Their looks quickly changed to anger as they ran towards him. The first soldier to reach him screamed as he swung his sword in a wide arc to the left. Kerr pivoted around the swipe and dealt a blow of his own, the head of his hammer crunching into the man's shoulder. The soldier stumbled forward, crying out as bones broke.

Kerr continued on towards the second soldier who made a lunge aimed at his ribs. Kerr used the handle of the hammer to slap the blade aside, then wrenched the handle back, aiming a little higher, colliding against the soldier's jaw. A couple of teeth flew out of his mouth in a spray of spit and blood.

He spun round just in time to evade a clumsy chop from the first soldier. The soldier stumbled forward, all his strength committed to the move. He hadn't expected Kerr to be able to turn in time to defend the attack. It left him wide open. With cruel force, Kerr drove the head of the hammer into his stomach, doubling him over. He followed it up with an overhead swing to the back of the soldier's head, caving in his skull with a wet crunch. Blood spattered Kerr's face.

A sharp pain suddenly lanced his side. The second soldier had recovered a lot quicker than he'd expected. The tip of his blade was coated with blood. Kerr staggered back, touching his side. He felt the wetness of warm blood on his fingers. It didn't feel deep – at least he hoped it wasn't.

As he retreated, he stumbled over a rock and landed on his ass, his hammer slipping from his grip. Cursing, he could only look up at the soldier as he raised his sword for the killing blow. He brought it down, Kerr closed his eyes. Then nothing, only the sound of a grunt coming from above him.

Kerr opened his eyes. The soldier had stopped mid-swing, a look of surprise etched across his face. He slowly looked down. Kerr followed his gaze. An arrow tip protruded from his chest. He dropped to his knees and landed face first next to him.

Rian stood a few yards in front of him, standing on a chimney which was lying on its side, bow held aloft. "Thought you could use a hand," she said, smiling, a little of her old self shining through.

"Where were you?" he asked, trying, and failing to keep a smile from forming on his lips.

"I was hiding just over there," she said, pointing behind her. "I saw you fight the men. When that one stabbed you, I thought

I'd pull you out of the shit."

They both stared at each other, then began to laugh. Amidst the bodies and the blood, it felt good to laugh with a friend.

He walked over to the dead men, wondering where they had come from. He noticed they wore the same black armour as the men he'd found in the clearing, days ago. He knelt down to get a closer look. Across the breast-plate was the image of a screaming skull. But it didn't look like a scream of fear, it looked more like a scream of fury, like it was shouting a battle-cry. Whatever it was, it gave him the creeps.

He turned to Rian. "Come on, lets..."

The world suddenly turned white with heat. He could feel himself being thrown back through the air and hitting something solid. His whole body became a cauldron of agony. Whatever he had collided with had knocked the air from his lungs. He lay on his side gasping in great heaves. Amidst his scrambled wits, he thought he could hear a scream, then scuffling, then the sound of a blow which silenced the screaming.

Rian.

His vision swam. He caught a glimpse of a blurred figure standing over him. He tried to get up, but his legs wouldn't comply. Then he felt hands pull him roughly to his feet.

"The war has just begun, Knight," a voice growled in his ear. "But for you it is nearly over. It awaits you at the ruined cottage. I will be waiting."

The blurred figure head-butted him, his head snapped back as he dropped to the ground.

He lay helpless on his side as he watched Rian's prone form hanging limply over the back of a horse as it was riding away from him towards the forest.

Chapter Fourteen - A Taste of One's Own Medicine

Lana lay in bed, listening to the sound of wood striking wood. The rhythmic clacking and occasional mutter told her Gren was practising in the yard, which meant his father would be in town for the day.

She threw back the thick sheets and rolled out of bed, feeling the satisfying cracks of her joints as she stretched. She reached over and poured herself some water from the jug on the bedside cabinet. Her thirst sated, she got up and tiptoed to the window, making sure she kept hidden behind the curtains.

From the small gap she peered through, she watched as he swung his stick at the block. Every now and again, between breaths, his gaze would wander up to her window – she wasn't sure what to make of that, probably self-conscious.

Or he knew she watched him, as she was sure he'd spotted her the day those two bullies had beat him up.

The thought of those two idiots began to sour her mood. They had no honour. Beating and mocking a smaller, younger boy, instead of passing on the lessons they'd obviously been taught. They had the look of high-born about them, with their fine clothes, and expensive looking practice blades. They probably thought this made them better than Gren and his family. It was absurd.

Watching Gren made her think of her father. He'd taught her how to fight and defend herself from a very young age. "A woman living in the real world must have the skills to defend herself, and not rely on a man for protection," he'd said, the thought of his stern teachings bringing a smile to her lips.

"Like mother?" she'd asked.

He'd chuckled, as his gaze lingered on her mother, hanging up their clothes behind them, a loving expression spread across his face. "Your mother can look after herself," he'd said, raising one eyebrow. "Don't you worry about that, girl."

The memory brought a fresh wave of sorrow to her heart, but it was mixed with happiness. She missed them so much. He'd imprinted the ideals of helping those who didn't have the courage or strength to help themselves. She smiled as Gren made a few more clumsy stabs at the block, then proceeded to shout at the block as though willing it to dare disagree with him.

She looked up. "I'll help him, father," she said aloud. "That's what you would do."

The loss of her parents still weighed heavily on her heart. It still felt like an open wound, catching her unawares when she least expected it. To think, just weeks ago she was helping her mother in the kitchen, or accompanying her father on a hunt, or a trip into the local villages. She thanked the Gods for Gren and his family. With their help she'd begun the slow process of healing.

She'd been pleased with herself she had managed to venture from her room a lot more. She'd started to regularly join Gren and his family for meals instead of eating alone in her room, wallowing in self-pity. She thought of the first night she'd joined them for dinner. There had been an awkward silence to begin with. From the furtive glances they made at each other, she surmised it was through fear of upsetting her and sending her up to her room in tears.

But as the days passed, she'd broken the silence, asking them about life on the farm. She found their stories interesting, and sometimes amusing. She thought they had a good life. Their little dynamic reminded her of home, with their little inside jokes and anecdotes. She'd thanked them for what they had done for her. June had waved her comment aside dismissively, stating it was what anyone would have done.

She thought of Gren. Shy at first and probably a little embarrassed from their first encounter on the riverbank, her knife held against his throat. The memory made her flush with shame and embarrassment. He had gradually come out of his shell, making her laugh and taking her mind momentarily off her woes.

The incident with the wolves played constantly on her mind as well. She hadn't been back to the woods since. She still couldn't wrap her head around what had happened that night. The image of them parting and bowing their heads as she passed filled her head with bemusement. The strange sensation in the pit of her stomach.

She shook the thought aside to tackle another day. She put her hands in the lukewarm bowl of water, June had left while she was sleeping, and splashed her face. She shrugged out of her shift and gave herself a quick wash, then dried herself and threw on a clean shirt and hose.

She left her room, and rushed downstairs, taking the steps two at a time. June was in the kitchen rolling dough for bread. She turned and gave Lana a smile. "Morning dear, would you like some breakfast?

Lana smiled and shook her head. "No thank you, June. Maybe later. Just need some fresh air." June smiled, her eyes glistening, and resumed rolling the dough.

She opened the front door, the heat from the noon sun bathing her with a pleasant warmth. She closed her eyes and took in a deep lungful of fresh country air, her nostrils filling with the aromas of cut grass, and pine from the forest.

She headed round the back of the house towards the faint sounds of wood striking wood. Gren had set up his practice block in front of the stables – giving him a good view of the main road, she noted. He had his back to her. She could hear him panting from the exertion of his wild, erratic swinging. She laughed internally in spite of herself. He looked like he was doing a bad job at cutting down a tree.

"You're doing it wrong," she said.

Surprised at the sudden interruption, Gren let the stick slip from his sweaty hand, and accidentally punched the block. The dull sound of his knuckles crunching against the wood suggested it hurt quite a bit.

"Bloody hell," he exclaimed in annoyance, which turned to surprise when he turned around and saw who was standing in front of him. "Lana. You're outside?"

She grinned at him, then looked up at the sky, feigning a look of surprise. "Yes. It appears you're right, Gren, I'm outside." She nodded at the block. "And you're doing it wrong. Your feet are in the wrong position and you swing that sword like you're cutting wheat."

Gren's cheeks reddened slightly. "How would you know?" he said, picking up the stick.

She shrugged. "Just telling you what I see."

He pursed his lips, his brow furrowing, as he retook his position. "Well it's not like father's going to send me up to the barracks, or hire a tutor to teach me the finer points of swordplay." He took another clumsy swing at the block. "So, this stick and that block are all I've got."

He resumed his onslaught on the block,

sulking a little. Lana hopped on the fence, deciding not to poke any more fun at him. She didn't want to be cruel, and it was clearly a sore point.

After an hour, Gren stopped, panting and sweating, and joined Lana on the fence. They didn't say anything, just enjoyed each other's company in silence.

Their peace was broken by the sound of voices coming from the road. Gren groaned. "Here we go again," he muttered under his breath.

Finn and Tom strode towards them, pointing and laughing. "Let your girlfriend out for a walk, huh Gren?" Finn said, winking at Lana. "How's your swordplay coming along? Fancy another lesson?" He vaulted the fence and drew his fine practice blade from its sheath.

Tom pushed Gren off the fence towards Finn, and sat next to Lana.

Gren loped towards Finn, who was spinning his blade in intricate arcs, like a man walking to the gallows.

"Come on, Gren. Let's show your girlfriend how a real man uses a sword," Finn said, boasting.

"Are they coming along later?" Gren asked. Lana giggled eliciting a sneer from Finn.

Without warning, Finn lunged at Gren with a swipe aimed at his neck. Gren only just managed to stumble back avoiding the blow by inches.

"Not getting any better, Gren, are we?" he said, grinning like a cat who'd cornered a mouse.

Gren swung his stick, aimed at Finn's head. Finn saw the move coming and easily manoeuvred around him, slapping Gren's backside with the flat of the blade sending him stumbling forward.

Finn laughed, clearly enjoying himself at Gren's expense. "Tell you what, soldier. If I best you, I get a kiss from your girlfriend," he said, winking at Lana. He really was repulsive.

Gren's face suddenly grew purple with rage. He flew at Finn in a fit of fury Lana had never seen before. "She's..." Miss "Not..." Swipe. "My..." Miss. "Girlfriend," he screamed.

Finn, initially caught off-guard, regained his composure. He ducked a swing aimed at his head, and replied by smashing the pommel of the practice blade into Gren's jaw. Gren's head snapped back as the force of the blow sent him hard onto his back.

Lana had been deciding when was the best time to intervene. It was now. She'd had enough of this charade. She jumped down from the fence, pulling Tom's foot up at the same time, sending him crashing backwards off the fence.

"Gren, are you alright?" she asked, running over to him.

Gren looked up at her groggily, rubbing his jaw. "I'm fine, Lana. Just a scratch."

Finn approached her, a look of triumph on his face. "Think I'm owed a kiss," he said, reaching for Lana's arm. Lana quickly picked up Gren's stick and swatted Finn's cheek with it. He stumbled back in surprise.

"Tell you what, if you can best me, you can get that kiss," she said.

Finn's expression changed. A predatory sneer spread across his face as his gaze wandered over her, making her skin crawl. His friend had picked himself off the flower bed, he pointed towards Lana. "Beat that little bitch, Finn. Teach her some respect."

Finn smiled as he began to circle her, spinning his sword, she presumed, in intimidation. "You sure? Hardly fair me armed with my fine blade, and you having that little thing." He stopped, and grinned. "But then again, if you're going out with Gren, you'll be used to handling little sticks." he said, which elicited a roar of laughter from his pathetic friend.

From the corner of her eye, she could see Gren's face turn a dark shade of scarlet. She smiled at the idiot. "I'll go easy on you."

He rushed in with a jab. She smiled inwardly. She'd seen the move coming before he'd decided to make it. His tells were shockingly obvious for one who'd supposedly had tutoring from the Lord's drillmasters.

This should be fun, she thought.

She spun gracefully around his attack and swatted the back of his neck, quickly following it up with a waspish lash to the back of the thighs. He yelped, hopping forward.

Tom started to laugh, but was quickly silenced by the glare his friend gave him.

"You little bitch," he shouted, swinging his blade at her head. It was the reaction she'd been expecting. As her father had taught her, if uncontrolled, anger could make you stupid in a fight. If the strike had connected, at the very least, it would have seriously injured her, practice blade or not. She wasn't worried. The boy was undisciplined.

Gren shrieked in dismay, probably thinking she wouldn't be able to avoid the blow in time.

Using a defensive technique she'd been taught, she bent backwards at the last moment, avoiding the swing. It was so close, she felt the wind caused by the blade as it passed inches above her head.

Finn had committed so much force into his wild slash, he hadn't expected to miss. It gave Lana the opening she needed.

Lana rose upright once more and grabbed the hair on the back of his neck. She drove her knee into his stomach, doubling him over. His precious practice blade slipped from his grasp. He wheezed as his breath escaped him. She kept hold of his hair and pulled him upright, slamming her palm into the bridge of his nose, breaking it. His head whipped back, sending a geyser of blood up and over his head, followed by a nasally whine.

She let him go, watching with grim satisfaction, as he staggered back spluttering incoherently through blood and snot, tears running down his face. She calmly picked up his practice sword, flipped it round so she was holding the end of the blunted blade, and swung it at his head. There was a sickening crack as the pommel cracked against the side of his face. He spun round and landed face first on the grass, unconscious.

"Lana," a voice screamed, behind her. She turned to find June staring wide eyed, and fearful at her. "What have you done?"

Her relish quickly turned to guilt and horror.

Finn's practice sword slipped from her grasp as she dropped to her knees. Her voice left her, she couldn't bear to look at the terrible expression of June's face any longer. She looked over at Gren. He stared at her wide eyed, his mouth hanging open in what looked like wonder.

Tom rushed over to his friend and picked him up. June rushed passed to help, but Tom slapped her hand away. "Leave it." He turned, and pointed to Lana. "You'll pay for this, bitch. You'll all pay for this."

Chapter Fifteen - The Last Knight of the Hour

Kerr chose each step with care as he approached the edge of the clearing in an effort to remain undetected. It was quiet. Too quiet for his liking. A mist had descended upon the forest, soaking him through. His shoulder hurt like hell, although the hot lances of pain had decreased to a dull throb which he thought was probably a good sign.

When he'd woken from the beating he'd been subjected to at the temple, he'd grabbed his belongings and ran in pursuit of Rian and her captor. He'd searched for his horse as it would aid in his haste to catch up to his friend and her captor, only to find the beast lying on her side by the road, her throat cut.

He'd been left with no choice but to follow their trail day and night, with no time to sleep. Images of his friend dying at the feet of whoever had taken her prevented him from slumber, urging him on.

He had to catch up to her. She was all he had left.

Another concern worrying at him was why he was still alive. He had no doubt whoever had taken her had something to do with the destruction of his home. He had a nagging feeling he was being toyed with.

He touched his injured shoulder. It was still a little tender. Not long after he had left the temple grounds, he'd cauterized the wound with a hot knife, his screams and shouts breaking the silence of the forest. He could have used his power, but knew that he would need every ounce of strength for the inevitable fight that lay ahead.

He felt tired, relying on the constant flow of adrenaline and reserves of power to keep going. He was sure of a battle. He just wasn't sure he'd come out the other end of it unscathed in his current state.

He unclipped his hammer, and pushed through the foliage into the open. There was no-one else there. He circled round the clearing, attuning his senses in anticipation of an ambush. He got halfway round when he found Rian, lying on her side with her hands and feet tied.

All thoughts of caution left him as he rushed over to her. "Rian," he said, dropping his hammer at his side, picking her up and cradling her in his arms. "Rian, are you alright? Say something. Anything."

She didn't move. He pulled his knife out from his belt and cut her bonds. He hovered his palm over her mouth, relieved to feel her faint breath on his skin.

He looked up at the night's sky. "Thank the Gods."

"The Gods won't help you here, Knight," a voice called at his back. "For there is only one God, and he's coming for you all."

Kerr cast his gaze in the direction of the voice. A man wearing the same armour as the men he'd killed at the temple stood before him. He wore a large gauntlet on his right hand. The screaming face on the breast-plate seemed to look straight at him. The man caught his gaze and smiled, touching the image tenderly.

"This is the face of the only God who matters, Knight." He pressed his hand flat against the image, a glassy, faraway look crossing his features. "The Fury will bind the land in blood, and rule with fear made of iron."

He thought he'd heard those words before, he just couldn't place when, or where. "The Fury?" he asked, raising an eyebrow.

The man nodded. "It is I who serves the Fury. As will the rest of this world, in time. He comes for us all."

Kerr narrowed his eyes at the man. "And you are?"

The man bowed, swiping his hand in a flourish. "I am Fargus, a soldier fighting in His name." He pointed towards the ruined cottage. "I was here when we destroyed this little hovel, rooting out your kind."

Kerr glanced over to the two graves where the two Knights of the Hour now resided. "And the temple? My brothers and sisters? How?"

Fargus laughed. "Your arrogance astounds me, Knight. It was easier than we could ever have comprehended. We knew the Hour had lost its way after all the centuries that had passed since the old wars.

Never in our wildest dreams could we have dreamed it was far worse than we had first anticipated."

Kerr looked down as Rian coughed. She didn't open her eyes, but her movements filled him with hope.

Fargus continued. "Decades ago the Fury planted an agent within the ranks of children to be trained at the temple, to be a Knight of the Hour. Over the coming years the agent planted strategic weaponry in specific locations within the temple. All my master had to do was wait for the right time." He chuckled. "It was so easy."

Kerr could feel anger grow within him like a spark to the pyre. "Why not kill me at the temple? Why lead me on this merry chase through the forest? I'm the last Knight of the Hour, why not be done with it?"

Fargus tilted his head to the side in amusement. "Seeing as you're the last of your ilk, I thought to have some fun."

Kerr dipped his head down at Rian. "And my friend? What happens to her?"

Fargus raised his eyebrows. "The Cleric? Yes, well I was going to just kill her, then I had a better idea." He began to pace in front of him "The crown want retribution for the death of King Hal. All fingers are currently pointed in the direction of the Hour. Initially that posed a dilemma, as you are the last Knight, and you will die here at my hands. But then I had a thought," he said, tapping a finger against his temple. "Instead of handing them a dead Knight, why not give them a live Cleric of the Hour to execute before the baying crowds, closing the matter."

Kerr gently laid Rian down and rose to his feet. "Over my dead body you will," he said, picking up the hammer.

Fargus smirked. "That's the idea."

Kerr took a few steps towards Fargus. "From where I'm standing, you're the enemy of the crown. What will you think King Skallen will make of the truth?"

Fargus laughed. "My dear Knight, who do you think helped endorse the destruction of your temple and drag the good name of the Hour through the mud? King Skallen is a lot easier to control and manipulate than his stubborn brother. A problem that was quickly resolved."

Everything was beginning to make sense. The King hadn't been the only one who'd known of his presence in the city, a loose end needing tending. His disagreement, and inevitable flight had been delicately orchestrated. The King's death not long after his exodus. Skallen's ascension to the throne. The destruction of his Order. How hadn't he seen this coming? He'd been too preoccupied with reaching the temple, blinded to the truth. It was leading up to something, he just didn't know what.

Fargus smiled as he watched Kerr put the pieces of the puzzle together. "Soon the Fury will change these lands forever. The Knights of the Hour scattered to the wind. Lost to history as a new age dawns."

"Who is this Fury? Where is he now? Is he with the King?" he asked. He was growing weary of this fanatic's self-righteous preaching.

Fargus raised his arms. "He is everywhere. He is here. He is in the palace, with the king. He was within your walls as your temple burned to the ground. He has waited many centuries to return." He pulled his sword from its sheath, pointing the blade at Kerr." The Knights of the Hour defeated him long ago, but they didn't fully destroy him. All He had to do was wait until events turned to stories, to myth, forgotten by your foolish High Lords."

Kerr raised his hammer. He'd heard enough talk from this fanatic. He took a step forward. "Now I know," he said, grinning.

"It matters not," Fargus said, raising the gauntlet. It glowed, then shot out a stream of the same burning white light that had struck him at the temple.

Kerr was ready this time. He brought the head of the hammer to meet the stream of light. To Fargus' surprise, the hammer consumed the light until it faded to nothing.

Not giving Fargus a moment to wrap his head around his weapon's failure to kill him, Kerr ran towards him and swung with all the rage burning through him.

Fargus blocked the swing – only just – sending sparks everywhere. He followed it with two strikes of his own. He was fast. Kerr blocked them, and made a kick at his shins causing Fargus to back up.

Already his shoulder felt as though it was on fire. He quickly glanced over at Rian, then to the two graves. He couldn't fall to this madman.

With lightning speed, he unsheathed his knife and threw it at Fargus, following it with a swing of the hammer. Fargus swatted the throwing knife aside, but was unable to fully dodge the hammer. Kerr heard a crunch as something broke. He spun and swiped the handle aimed at Fargus' neck. Fargus rolled out of the way avoiding the strike by inches.

They stood facing each other, panting. From the look on Fargus' face, he'd underestimated him. Kerr rushed in once more. They circled the clearing trading blow for blow, never giving an inch. For that would mean death for either of them. A mild panic began to gnaw at him. He could feel himself begin to tire, were Fargus, despite the injury he'd caused to his arm, seemed to be getting stronger, faster.

Fargus sensed his doubt and began to press more aggressively. As the fight drew on, Kerr began to suffer a cut or wound from every third or fourth of Fargus' attacks. He could feel his blood running down from the various wounds he'd taken. He had to kill this maniac. He was the last Knight of the Hour.

He was also running out of his vastly

depleting power just to keep up with Fargus. He'd never fought anyone this strong before. The fanatic was just too quick for the hammer. He had to get in at close quarters if he stood a chance.

He still had his other knife.

An idea came to him as their battle edged towards the outer edges of the clearing. It was the only way he could get close enough to strike a killing blow.

He stumbled back, luring Fargus closer towards the tree-line. He suffered a few more cuts a little deeper than before as they drew closer to the trees.

He didn't have much time. It was now or never.

He looked over at Rian. She wouldn't forgive him for what he was about to do – he just hoped she wasn't too unconscious. Fargus sliced at him, Kerr blocked, but let the hammer skitter from his grasp deliberately. Fargus grinned in triumph.

Kerr looked over at Rian, "I'm sorry, Rian. It's up to you," he said, opening his arms.

Fargus didn't hesitate. He drove his sword with all his rage through his stomach and out of his back, missing his spine by a couple of inches. The sword continued on into the tree behind him, pinning him. He felt a coldness inside, and heat on the outside as blood ran down from the wound.

Kerr used the last vestige of strength he had left and gripped Fargus' hand, still holding the hilt. With his free hand he pulled his knife out and drove it through Fargus' eye, and out the back of his head.

For a moment, Fargus' mouth opened in surprise, but no words came out. Kerr let him drop with his blade still embedded in his head.

He could taste blood in his mouth, the taste of it bitter on his tongue. Pinned to the tree, he looked over to Rian, who was beginning to stir.

He smiled as his eyes began to close.

Chapter Sixteen – Summons

Lana stared through the window. The sky was grey and dull, matching her mood. She'd barely remembered getting up. She focused on her faint reflection on the glass. Her hair was a mess, it hung in rats' tails, covering half of her face. She blew at a strand near her mouth. She picked up a brush and made a half-hearted attempt to comb out the knots, her head jerking to the side whenever she pulled at a particularly tangled section of hair.

She sighed, putting the brush down and giving up. She laid her hands on the varnished surface of the dresser. What a miserable morning, she thought. Was it morning? She wasn't sure. Her sleeping patterns were still all over the place.

It wasn't the only thing that was all over the place, she thought. She found her grief came in unexpected waves, seemingly without a care for when it struck, whether she be at the table eating a piece of the lovely bread Gren's mother baked, or on the privy, or in the yard.

She thought about the incident in the yard. She had to admit, it had felt good to teach those two bullies a lesson. She smiled at the image of Finn's nose exploding, blood and snot flying. Her smile faltered as she remembered the horrified look on June's face after she'd just witnessed the beating she'd given Finn. The memory made her cringe with shame.

It made her think of her father. She was sure he would have been proud of her. She'd put into practice the lessons and ideals he'd spent years teaching her; defending the weak, respecting honour. He'd also taught her patience – though she knew she struggled with that at times.

She smiled, which surprised her, given that any other time she thought of him would have her in tears. Not giving her grief time to rear its ugly head, she got up and gave herself a quick wash in the water bowl. She picked up the shirt she'd worn the previous day and brought it up to her nose, it didn't smell too bad. She threw it over her head, pulled on her hose and shoes, and ventured downstairs.

She bound into the kitchen to find Gren sitting at the dining table, his mother and father sat either side of him. It was unusually quiet – never a good sign, she thought. Gren wore his default expression; anxious. June smiled at her, though she noticed it didn't reach her eyes. His father, Steven, stared blankly at her.

"Is there something the matter?" she asked, already knowing the answer.

June raised a hand, gesturing towards the empty chair beside her. "Lana, dear. Could you take a seat," she said, softly. Lana nodded and sat down.

Steven clasped his hands together and

leaned forward. He slowly turned his head around to face her. He smelled of sweat and horses, a smell she didn't find all that unpleasant. "Lana. We're sorry for all the troubles you've been through, we really are. If our Gren hadn't found you when he did, who knows what might have happened to you by the riverbank. You've been more then helpful around the farm, and we're happy for you to stay with us for as long as you need."

She mumbled a thank you. He nodded, and continued. "It's just... as you can no doubt guess, me and June would like to have a word with you about what happened in the yard with those two boys, a week back.

Those boys are the sons of two of the Lord's personal guard. I was in the market yesterday when young Simon, the butcher's boy, told me he'd been up to the keep the day before and learned that the two guards have petitioned for your arrest." He turned to Gren. "The both of you."

Gren opened his mouth then closed it as his father raised a hand. "Let me finish. Before this gets out of hand, I would suggest the two of you take a walk up to the keep and apologise for the trouble you've caused."

Gren slammed a hand on the table, startling them all. "Horseshit. Finn and Tom started it. They had no right to come into our yard and..."

"That's beside the point, Gren," Steven snapped at his son. "You shouldn't have been in the yard anyway." He narrowed his eyes at Gren. "You should have been up at the ridge mending the fence like I'd told you to do. Instead you were swinging a stick at a block of wood, too busy playing soldier, instead of doing your chores."

Gren's look of outrage crumbled to that of shock as his father pressed the issue. "Don't think I didn't know what you were up to whenever I went into town." Gren's eyes flitted to his mother in accusation which his father noticed. "Before you accuse your mother, I found your practice instruments behind the stables when I was mucking them out."

Gren looked down at the table in shame. June placed a hand on her husband's and turned to Lana. "What we're saying, dear, is that it would be a good idea to straighten this horrible business before it grows arms and legs. We rent this land from Lord Cunningham, the last thing we want is to suffer his ire over something so trivial.

Lana doubted a boy like Finn would agree with June, especially with his face black and blue. Though she could see where Gren's parents were coming from. If she was being honest, she hadn't thought about the consequences her actions would cause. Looking at the pair of them, she felt her guilt increase.

She opened her mouth, ready to acquiesce to their demands, when Gren rose from his chair, throwing it back against the wall, his face red with fury. "I will be damned if we're going up there and beg the Lord's forgiveness for giving those two idiots a taste of their own medicine," he shouted.

"Don't speak to us in that disrespectful tone," Steven barked as Gren turned to leave. "We're not done, Gren. Not by a long shot. Sit back down this instance," he ordered his son.

Gren turned back to face his father, resting his hands on the table. He didn't sit back down. "Father, we shouldn't have to put up with bullies, then apologise for defending ourselves. It's not right. We're going for a walk," he said, walking round the table, taking Lana's hand, and storming out, taking a her with him, slamming the door in their wake.

~

They walked for the first couple of miles in silence – she thought it best if Gren used the time to simmer down from his altercation with his parents.

In the short time she'd known him, she'd never seen him talk back to his parents in that manner. There was a fire within him bubbling just beneath the surface.

As they came closer to the city gates, she noticed more than a few people staring, or pointing in their direction. She assumed more than just the butcher's boy now knew of the incident at Gren's.

They passed through the gates and took at

a seat on the wall surrounding the water fountain at the market square. Shops and stalls ringed around it, with people flitting in and around them buying whatever was for sale. Watching the hustle bustle of the market brought an odd sort of peace to her. She found the feeling pleasant.

The clouds had broken, leaving a warmness to the afternoon. Children splashed and played in the fountain to keep cool as their parents looked on. It was nice. She turned to Gren, who seemed oblivious to everything around him. His face was screwed up in thought. He'd probably been playing the argument on a loop since he'd slammed the front door behind them.

Deciding the silence had dragged on long enough, she nudged him breaking him from his internal torture. "You do realise it was just me that beat up Finn," she said, playfully. He muttered something under his breath, then resumed his sullen brooding.

She thought a change of tact was in order. She nudged him once more. "Your parents are right, you know."

It had the desired effect. He shot up from his seat, as though something had bitten his backside. He turned to face her, his face going redder with rage by the second. "You're taking their side? You?" he shouted, not caring his outburst had garnered more than a few stares.

She nodded. "Yes, me." She paused a moment in case he had something more to add. He didn't. "Your parents are farmers, Gren. They rent the land from the Lord whose men their son's friend assaulted. They may be just trainees, but in my book, they still count as his men. The last thing June and Steven want is to cause offence and insult to his soldiers, causing unnecessary grief within his ranks. Now I agree those two fools needed taking down a peg or two, though the manner in which it happened wasn't anywhere near the best approach for which I apologise. I let my anger get the better of me. You and your family have looked after me, the last thing I want is to cause you any problems."

His features softened. He sighed and sat down beside her. "You have nothing to apologise for, Lana. What you did that day was amazing. I would love to be able to fight like that. Finn's a lot bigger than you, but you whipped his ass as though he was half your size. Where did you learn to..."? He trailed off as the grief must have swept across her face. He lowered his head. "Lana, I'm sorry. I didn't mean to..."

She got up and put a hand on his shoulder. "It's okay. My father taught me, when I was very young." She sat back down. "Let's just enjoy the afternoon without thinking about what's happened. We can deal with it later." He smiled and nodded.

They sat for a while, enjoying each other's company while the townsfolk went about their business around them. Their reverie was broken by a huge splash behind them which soaked Gren and completely missed Lana.

Gren shrieked, jumping up from his seat and turning to find the one responsible for soaking him. A girl around Gren's age, stood smiling at him mischievously without the slightest care her fine clothes were soaking wet. "Gren," she exclaimed. "You're soaked through."

Gren's look of outrage was somewhat spoiled by his inability to hide the smile that spread across his face. "Marissa, why in God's name would you do that?"

The girl called Marissa cupped a handful of water and threw it towards him, laughing. "Because it's too hot, and it's fun to see your face all pinched and screwed up like you've just bitten a lemon."

Laughing herself at Gren's discomfort, which seemed to have erased the day's tension, cupped a handful and threw it at him.

"Lana, quit it," he spluttered, as the water splashed his face.

Marissa smiled at Lana. "You must be the fighter Gren found on the riverbank." She paused, looking her up and down. "He did say you were pretty."

Gren turned a deep shade of purple. "I did not say that, Rissa."

Marissa raised an eyebrow at him. "So, she's not pretty?"

"Well yes, she is pretty, but I didn't say

she...What are you doing here?" he asked, giving up.

Marissa feigned shock. "Well my father is Lord of this city, and its surrounding lands." Lana's smile faltered at the mention of the Lord, Marissa caught her look and began to shake her head. "Don't worry, Lana. If my father knew I was talking to the two of you, he'd kill me. Gren's my friend. Besides, it matters not, he's always annoyed with me anyway."

"What for?" Lana asked.

"I'm not a boy," she said, giggling, but Lana could sense a sad bitterness in the tone of her voice. "I came here to warn you."

"Warn us of what?" they asked in unison.

She nodded behind them. "Too late," she said, turning and vaulting the fountain wall, disappearing into the crowd.

Lana and Gren turned as the thunder of hoofs grew louder. People began to spill out of the way as two mailed riders approached them, halting a few feet in front of them. The rider closest raised his visor to reveal a scowling face that looked down at them with nothing short of contempt. "The two of you will accompany us to the keep, on orders of Lord Cunningham."

Chapter Seventeen – Reprimanded

Lana thumped up and down in the saddle as the soldier pushed the horse at speed through the town, heading for the Lord's keep. Her bones felt like they were rattling about in a bag. She bit her tongue for the second time, aiming a curse in the direction of her chaperone – who either didn't hear, or didn't care.

She cast a sidelong glance at Gren. His face was chalk white, he appeared to be muttering to himself – she presumed he was trying to convince himself their situation wasn't as bleak as it seemed. His expression suggested he doubted it very much. She caught his eye and gave him a weak smile which he reluctantly returned.

Much like Gren, she was more than a little concerned herself. Although she had more or less stated to Gren this was the correct course of action. She grew more dubious the closer they came to the Lord's keep, continually going over their argument in her head.

Finn and Tom had deserved what they got. As they galloped up to the hill, she thought it obviously served them well being sons of men tasked with guarding the Lord of these lands. She had no doubts it was one of the main reasons they felt they could get away with bullying whoever they wanted.

As they turned a corner, the archway

which led into the keep came into view. She sighed, it seemed some people thought they were above the laws of men.

They passed under the arch. Two men, armed with crossbows, looked down at them as they went. One of them shouted back something towards the main courtyard. She thought it sounded like 'they're here'.

They halted abruptly at the foot of the steps leading into the keep, causing Lana to jolt forward clattering her face against the mail of the guard in front. Stable boys rushed over to them, taking the reins. Lana's chaperone slid down from the saddle, turned and pulled her down a little rougher than she'd been expecting.

"Thanks," she said, sarcastically.

The soldier pushed her towards the steps. "In there. The Lord's waiting."

Gren fell into step beside her as they ascended the stone stairs, and entered Lord Cunningham's keep, the soldiers following closely at their backs.

"What do you think's going to happen to us?" Gren whispered.

If she was being honest, she had about as much of a clue as Gren did. One thing that was bothering her, and had been the moment they had been arrested at the fountain, was why the Lord himself was dealing with a disagreement between a bunch of kids. Surely a ticking off from the local guard, or a meeting between the parents would've sufficed. Wouldn't it? She smiled at Gren.

"It'll be fine," she said, attempting to assure him. Though she was hardly convinced herself.

They entered the main hall where Lord Cunningham was seated on a huge throne up on a stone dais. She was beginning to have a very bad feeling about this.

They stopped and bowed to the Lord of Dalton's Hill. He smiled down at them, dipping his head a touch. She noticed Gren seem to relax a little at the Lord's expression. To Lana it looked like the smile of a snake. She noted Marissa looked nothing like her father. Where he was short and stocky, Marissa was tall and lithe. She must favour her mother – lucky her, she thought.

"Dear children," Cunningham said, clapping his hands together. The sound echoing around the circular hall. "What am I to do with you?" He got up and walked down from the dais towards them. He waved a hand dismissively at the two guards. "That will be all, gentlemen, I'm sure your Lord is in no mortal peril, regardless of the girl's ability to easily subdue a trainee of the Dalton guard." She noticed his eyes narrowed a fraction amidst his cheery expression. It made her feel a little uneasy.

The guards saluted and left without a word. One of them did pause for a second longer than the other, as though he were about to add something, then thought better of it.

Lana watched them as they left, closing

the doors behind them. She turned to find Lord Cunningham silently appraising her. He smiled that smile she didn't fully trust. He nodded behind her, raising his eyebrows. "You must forgive Oliver, my dear. His son was the boy you had the altercation with; Finn. He feels somewhat embarrassed by the unfortunate turn of events."

She turned to Gren, who was currently fascinated by his shoes. Lord Cunningham laughed a great bellow, making the jowls under his chin jiggle. "The look on your faces." He shook his head. "Were you expecting me to throw you in the dungeons, or cast you out of my lands? For fighting with boys your own age? When I was your age I was always falling in and out of scraps." From the look of him, she had trouble believing he'd ever been in a fight in his life, but she kept that thought to herself.

"Then why have us brought up to your keep by armed soldiers, if the matter is so trivial," she asked, before she could stop the words spilling from her mouth.

Gren whipped his head round and gave her a look of dread. She caught the slightest flicker of irritation cross Cunningham's face, then it was gone. "Intrigue, my dear," he said. "Intrigue. Yours is an interesting tale. A young girl found half dead by our Gren on the riverbank, with fighting skills most unusual for someone your age, and I hope you take no offence, but your sex. Tell me, Lana, where are your parents? They must be worried sick."

The mention of her parents caused her throat to tighten. Her vision blurred at the edges as tears began to well in the corners of her eyes. She lowered her head, closing her eyes in an effort to push back feelings still a little raw from the surface. She took a deep breath and looked back up at the Lord, staring him in the eye. "They're dead."

The Lord shook his head, his brow furrowed. "My dear, forgive me." He stepped forward and put a clammy hand on her shoulder. She fought the urge to slap it away. "I'm sorry for your loss. Such tragic circumstances. You were fortunate young Gren found you when he did."

At the mention of his name, Gren found some courage to speak. "It was my fault, my Lord. I was practising in the yard when Finn and Tom jumped me. Lana was just helping."

Cunningham nodded, considering Gren's words. "I see. That is not how I have heard it. The boys, and their fathers, have stated it was the two of you who had started it, confronting them when they were on their way back from training at my keep. Now who am I to believe?" Gren opened his mouth to speak, but Cunningham raised a hand, a stern expression crossing his features, silencing Gren. "It matters not either way. I don't think your father would approve of you shirking your chores with silly games."

Gren looked back down at his feet. "He wasn't best pleased, my Lord. We had a falling out the last we spoke."

"Which will be remedied the next you speak, I do not doubt," he said, raising a questioning eyebrow. Gren mumbled something resembling his acquiescence. "Thus, bringing me to the question of what to do with the pair of you."

Lana began to speak, but the Lord raised his hand, smiling. "The fault is with the boys, regardless of who started it. Trainees of my guard have a duty to protect my wards, not fight them. I have already decided their punishment. They will muck out my stables for a week." Gren brightened at the Lord's judgement. Lana wasn't so sure.

"As for you, Gren, I would suggest you leave the swordplay to the men at my barracks. I think your father would agree with me, your place is by his side on the farm."

Gren nodded, the smile faltering on his lips. "Yes, my Lord," he mumbled.

The Lord turned to Lana. "As for you, my dear. You will be escorted to Oakhaven. You appear to me to be in perfect health. Lord Caster is currently understaffed. I will send a raven informing him I am sending an able-bodied girl in need of work, and permanent residence."

Lana felt as though she had been punched in the gut. The air escaped her, making her feel light-headed. She was to leave Gren and his family? Since her parents' death, they had been the only semblance of normalcy in her life. Gren stared at her mouth agape.

Her throat felt dry. Before she could attempt to croak a reply, Lord Cunningham turned and walked back up the dais. He rang a bell sitting on the table next to his throne. The guards entered. From the smile on Finn's father's face, she presumed they'd heard every word from the other side of the door.

Cunningham waved his hand in a flourish. "Escort young Gren back to his parents. Give them my regards and assure them the matter has been resolved. There will be no more repercussions." He looked down at them. "Now say your goodbyes. I'm sure, in time, you will see each other again."

Lana barely heard the Lord. She turned to Gren, tears streaming freely down her cheeks, and embraced him fiercely. She'd lost one family, now she was losing another. Was she destined to live her life alone?

"We'll see each other again," he whispered hoarsely in her ear. "I promise."

He let go, and was escorted from the hall. The doors shut with a bang, leaving her alone in the world once more.

~

Gren walked down the cold stone corridor in a mild haze. He'd arrived fully expecting the worst. But this was worse than anything he could ever imagine. The dungeons would have been better than this. He hadn't expected the Lord to send her to the capital, especially after he'd jested about not casting them from his lands.

What did he call this?

It wasn't right. It wasn't fair. And it was all because of Finn and Tom – though mostly Finn, Tom just followed Finn's lead. The thought made his blood boil with anger. He bunched his fists as he struggled to contain his rage.

Oliver pushed him forward, breaking him from his reverie. "Pick up the pace, Gren. That little bitch deserved a lot more for what she did to my boy." He snorted to the other guard. "A cosy job and a place to stay in the capital. Not bad for assault, if you ask me. You're both lucky our Lord has a forgiving nature."

"No-one's asking your opinion. And your boy is an ass," Gren said, before he could stop himself.

His head jerked forward as Oliver's gauntlet struck the back of his head. He stumbled forward, clattering to the ground, grazing his palms.

"Insolent boy. You should know your place. Don't think I'll forget this." He grabbed him roughly by the collar, and pulled him to his feet. "Now pick up the pace. We're taking you home to that hovel you call a home."

Gren didn't answer as he was pushed on.

He walked in silence, tears streaming down his face.

~

Lana stared at the door, listening as the sounds of her friend's footsteps disappeared down the hall behind the door, fading to nothing.

"Why?" she asked, turning to face the Lord.

Cunningham sat in his garish throne, a hint of teeth showing between his thin lips. "Why? Because these are my lands, filled with my people." He leaned forward, smiling. Though this smile was anything but pleasant. "And you aren't one of my people. I find it suspicious you appeared on my lands, in my city, not long after the temple was destroyed, and our sovereign murdered."

She felt she was bearing witness to the real Lord Cunningham. A Lord who would play with people's lives as he saw fit, to scorn his daughter for being a daughter.

"I was attacked. My mother and father murdered. I barely escaped with my life. Gren and his family saved me. I don't know anything about the temple. Who destroyed it? Who murdered King Hal?"

Cunningham leaned forward. "I was hoping you would tell me. Where did you say your home was?"

"I didn't," she said, her voice rising in

anger.

"Don't play games with me, child. Who was your father? Was he a Knight of the Hour? From what I've been told of your fighting skills, you don't learn that just anywhere."

She thought back to that terrible night in the clearing. The man in the black armour had called her father a Knight. She felt like she was being handed pieces to the wrong jigsaw puzzle.

She considered her next words carefully. She didn't trust Cunningham. Not one bit. Something felt wrong. She couldn't make sense of what was going on. "My father was a ranger. We lived in the forest to the west, near the mountain border. Men in black armour came to my home, murdered my parents, and chased me off a cliff." She negated to mention the flash of light, and explosion that had thrown her off the cliff.

The Lord leaned forward. His eyes narrowed in suspicion. "Hmm, is that so?" He nodded slowly, clearly not convinced. "It matters not to me, though I think the truth will come out eventually."

Lana crossed her arms. "I suppose your friend, Lord Caster, will be questioning me as well?"

Cunningham laughed at this. "Lord no, my dear. There is no 'Lord Caster'. There's no job, or residence where you're going. I just said that to get that stupid boy out of my sight." He glanced behind her. "What happens to you now is of no concern to me. Isn't that right, Captain?"

Lana felt a presence at her back she hadn't felt only moments before. Slowly, she turned around to be faced with the image of all her nightmares. The man in black armour stood in front of her, a cruel grin spread across his face. Amidst her horror, she was drawn to the ruined eye where her father had stabbed him.

"Lana, we meet again," he said, cheerily.

Her horror turned to fury. She screamed and threw herself at him, aiming to claw his other eye out of its socket. The grin remained as he quickly raised his gauntlet, and shot her in the chest with a blast of white light.

Her chest erupted in unspeakable agony as she was thrown across the room, crashing into one of the stone pillars, and clattering through a nearby table. She lay there, unable to move. Her body felt like it was ablaze.

Her vision blurred and swam, as she slowly climbed to her feet. She could see him approach her as she swayed, struggling to keep upright. His lips were moving, but she couldn't make out what he was saying aside from a dull drone. Her ears were ringing a continuous note, rendering everything else inaudible.

She watched, helpless, as he raised the gauntlet once more, and filled her vision with white light.

Then the world went black.

~

Marissa watched in stunned horror as the chambers lit up with the strange light from Argon's gauntlet once more. It struck Lana again, sending her flying back against the pillar for a second time. Only this time she never got up. She'd screamed, but there had been so much noise no-one had heard her. Was she dead?

Argon picked Lana up as though she weighed nothing, and hoisted her over his shoulder.

"Is she dead?" her father asked.

Argon shook his head. "Just unconscious. Such rage for one so young." He chuckled, the horrible sound of his laughter filling the room. Marissa felt as though she was going to be sick.

"Wouldn't it be better to just kill her and be done with it? My men could make the body disappear," her father said.

She covered her mouth in revulsion. She knew her father wasn't a particularly nice man. But this…

Argon shook his head once more. "No. You've played your part well, Lord Cunningham." He patted Lana's lifeless body. "I have plans for this one."

Her father shrugged, his expression devoid of any shred of empathy. "Be sure to tell your master my part in the proceedings. I have twelve, or so, men ready at the rear of the keep. They'll provide you with all you need."

Argon nodded, carrying Lana's lifeless body from the room, leaving her father alone.

Marissa ran from the balcony, down the stairs, and burst through a side door to her father's chambers pointing a finger at him. "How could you sit there and let that monster do that?" she screamed at him. "She's just lost her family. What has Lana got to do with anything? She was staying with Gren and his family when the King died."

In an uncharacteristic burst of speed, her father rushed down from his dais, and slapped her hard across the face, sending her down hard onto the stone floor, causing her to bite her lip in the process. She held a hand to her jaw, which had begun to throb. She could taste blood in her mouth.

Her father loomed over her, his face purple with rage. "You insolent little bitch, how dare you speak to your father, your Lord in such a disrespectful tone. How long have you been spying on me?"

She scowled up at him, defiant. He'd never struck her before. She could feel tears begin to form in the corner of her eyes. She wouldn't cry in front of him, though. She wouldn't give him the satisfaction.

"Long enough," she said, sounding more confident than she felt. She'd never been more terrified in her life.

He knelt down and grabbed her roughly by the jaw, causing her to yelp in pain. He pulled her close so she could smell the stale wine on his breath. She wanted to retch her guts up. "Now listen to me, daughter." He spat the last word out like it was bile. "I'm dealing with matters above the station of a silly little girl. You will leave my sight and forget everything you have seen. The sooner I take a new bride and put an heir in her. A male heir. The sooner I will be able to get a night's sleep without having to worry about my lands passing to a woman."

He pushed her face back and stormed out of the hall as it filled with the sounds of her sobs.

Chapter Eighteen – Roth

Gren's head bobbed as his horse ambled along the road. They had passed under the stone arch, leaving the city, a mile or so age. His mind was a fog, worrying over Lana, and where she was headed. They'd only been separated an hour, but he found be missed her already.

"Halt," Oliver called, behind him. Gren slowed his mount to a stop, and turned her around.

Gren looked at the guard, his face screwing in confusion. "Is there a problem? It's still a couple of miles until we reach the farm."

Oliver smiled a toothy grin. "I've changed my mind. After all the trouble you've caused, a long walk is exactly what you need. Take the time to think about what you and that little whore have done."

Rage engulfed him at the insult aimed at his friend. He pointed a finger at the two men. "You bring shame to the guard."

Oliver's smile faltered. He cantered his horse over to him, so they were side on, and elbowed him across the jaw, sending him tumbling from his saddle and into the mud.

Oliver took the reins of the now rider-less horse, guiding her to face the direction of the city. "Piss off home you li..." His insult was cut short as a large boulder struck his helm. His head jerked awkwardly to the side as it rung, and was sent clattering to the ground in a flailing pile of iron.

Before his comrade could react, a robed figure appeared as though from nowhere, pulling the dumbstruck soldier from his saddle. Gren couldn't see his face as it was hidden within the darkness of his hood. The soldier tried to climb to his feet to face his attacker, but the hooded man quickly pulled a sword from within his robes and smacked him on the head with the flat of the blade. He dropped and remained still.

Oliver had managed to climb back to his feet, his sword unsheathed ready to face the hooded man. "How dare you assault a Lord's man. An attack on his man is an attack on the Lord himself."

Gren could hear a snort from within the hood. "Well if that's the way of it, the Lord's going to receive a sore one." He turned to Gren, who'd remained sitting in the mud, his mouth agape. "Are you alright, my boy? That looked like a terrible tumble."

Gren nodded like an idiot. The hooded man replied with a nod of his own, then turned back to Oliver.

"You'll die for this, vagrant," Oliver shouted, quickly taking two steps forward, and swinging the sword at the hooded man's neck.

The hooded man didn't immediately move from the slash. Gren winced, expecting to see the hooded man's head cut off in front of him. But at the last second, in a fit of speed Gren had never witnessed, the hooded man rushed in close, towards Oliver trapping both his hands – and his sword – under his armpit.

Oliver glanced down and tried to wrench his weapon free. The hooded man drove his head into the opening of his helm. Gren heard a sickening crack as Oliver's head snapped back, blood and teeth spraying into the air.

They remained still for a couple of seconds, like a macabre statue. Oliver lowered his ruined face to meet the darkness of the hood, then his consciousness bailed on him, and he dropped to the ground like a sack of spuds.

Gren sat there in the mud, utterly amazed at the speed in which this strange figure had dispatched two of the Lord's personal guard.

Less than a minute ago, he'd been sitting on his horse.

He was suddenly aware of the hooded man standing over him. His sword was gone, which made Gren feel a little easier. He looked up at him.

"You'll catch flies if you keep that mouth open any longer, son," the hooded man said, a hint of amusement in his voice.

Gren managed to scrape together enough of his wits to speak. "Are you a Knight of the Hour?" he asked.

He couldn't see the hooded man's reaction to the question. He didn't answer, opting instead to help Gren to his feet.

"Why did you help me?" Gren asked.

The hooded man glanced over at the two unconscious soldiers and sighed. "Bullies dressed as guards are still just bullies. You were right to call out their shame."

Gren nodded, not knowing what else to say. The hooded man was right. They were bullies. He looked at Oliver and thought of Finn – like father, like son. This would come back to haunt him, he just knew it.

He turned to the hooded man. "The Lord won't be happy you beat up his men," he said, growing more and more worried at the thought of standing in front of the Lord once more. Another incident to answer for. Two incidents he had been a mere spectator to, he thought sourly.

The hooded man nodded. "I don't doubt it." He removed the hood and glanced towards the keep sitting proudly on top of the hill. He was older than he expected, given the speed he'd displayed, fighting the guards. His hair was cut short and mostly grey. His face looked weather-beaten, and tired. Looking into his eyes, he thought they looked sad. Like he'd lost something, never to return.

The man met Gren's gaze, and smiled grimly. "Dark times are coming, son. Lords and their soldiers who don't take care of their wards will be swept away with the tide." He sighed. "Come on, I'll accompany you to your home, I assume that's where the guards were escorting you to?"

Gren nodded, not having the faintest idea what he was going on about regarding tides, and being swept away. They were miles from the sea.

"I'm Gren, by the way. Nice to meet you."

The man laughed, and smiled down at him. "Nice to meet you, Gren. I'm Roth."

~

They ate up a couple of miles in silence, enjoying the cool breeze, a welcome relief from the heat of the afternoon sun. His jaw hurt like hell, but the image of Roth driving his head into Oliver's face made it easier to cope with. He laughed, which ironically caused his jaw to hurt.

"What's so funny," Roth asked.

Gren shook his head. "Nothing. Just thinking of the goofy look Oliver gave you after you'd head-butted him."

Roth laughed, a deep booming chuckle. "I think you'd look like that after having this slammed into your face," he said, patting his forehead. "So apart from making trouble with soldiers of the Lord, what do you do, Gren?"

"I help my mother and father on our farm," he said, still chuckling himself. "I have a small boat too, back at the harbour. It used to belong to my grandfather, before he died a few years ago. He'd always liked fishing, though I'd wager he was better at it than me. I'm not very good at it."

"Do you enjoy fishing?" Roth asked, sounding genuinely interested.

The question made Gren think of the jokes made at his expense whenever he came back with nothing in his basket. As much as it made him feel disappointed, it never stopped him going out again and again. On the days Finn and Tom weren't around, due to them training, he found he loved spending hours alone in his boat. He was surrounded by beautiful scenery and the peaceful quiet.

"Yes, I do," he said.

"Then that's all that matters," Roth said, clapping him on the shoulder. "It's good for the soul to spend at least one day a week doing something that brings you a little peace." His face darkened. "Those days will be far and few between soon." He didn't elaborate on his meaning, which concerned him a little.

"What about you? What brings you peace?" he asked. He found he liked this strange man with the sad eyes – despite the terrible violence. Lately people like that seemed to gravitate towards him. He thought of Lana, and quickly pushed the sadness he felt to the back of his mind for the moment.

Roth closed his eyes. He looked tired. He gave Gren a weak smile. "I haven't found peace in a long time."

Gren glance at Roth's robes, and thought of the sword he carried hidden beneath them. "Are you a Knight?" he asked.

"What makes you ask?"

"I dunno. The Robes. The sword. The way you handed Oliver his ass."

Roth chuckled. "I suppose I am, after a fashion. I've been away from these lands a long time."

"I heard the temple was destroyed," Gren said. Roth's jaw set at the comment. Gren cursed inwardly at himself for his bluntness. He opened his mouth to apologise, when the sound of hurried footsteps grew louder at their backs.

They both turned, expecting Oliver and his comrade, then dismissed the idea as the sound wasn't loud enough. The two soldiers were both wearing mail, and had two horse's nearby.

Marissa ran towards them, shouting his name. She skidded to a halt, panting and covered in sweat. Had she ran all the way from the keep? Her eyes were puffy and bloodshot, as though she had been crying. He also didn't fail to notice the nasty looking bruise on her cheek.

"Rissa, are you alright?" he asked, running over to her. He raised a hand up to her face. "What happened to your face?"

She slapped his hand away making him flinch. She caught his look of shock, and grabbed his hand. "It's nothing, I..." she paused, glancing over his shoulder. "Who's your friend? I passed the two unconscious guards that had escorted you from my father's keep. They looked like they'd been assaulted by a dozen men."

"Oh, that was Roth," he said, gesturing towards the robed man. "This is Roth, by the way. Oliver and his... Hang on, how do you know who escorted me from the keep?"

She shook her head emphatically, still struggling to catch her breath. "That's why I'm here. It's Lana," she exclaimed.

Gren raised his eyebrows in concern. "What's wrong? Is she okay? Did something happen to her up at the keep?" he said, glancing down at the bruise on her face.

"Did you say Lana?" Roth asked, his eyes narrowing.

Gren turned to the robed man. "I found her on the riverbank a few weeks ago. Her parents had been murdered. She escaped by falling in…"

Roth rushed over, and grabbed him by the shirt, spinning him round out of Marissa's grip. "What happened at the keep? Why was she there?" he shouted, a tone of panic to his voice. His eyes were as wide as saucers. They looked a little crazy, which frightened him.

Marissa grabbed at Roth's arm, trying to wrench it free of Gren's shirt. She may as well have been pulling at stone. "Hey, let him go," she screamed.

Roth seemed to collect himself at the sound of Marissa's screaming. He let go of Gren and faced Marissa. She took a step back, wary. He held up his hands, palms out. "I'm sorry. Look girl, we don't have time.

There are bad men after that girl."

Marissa crossed her arms at the robed man. "From where I'm standing, there's a bad man standing in front of me. You could be in league with him."

"With who?" Gren and Roth asked, in unison.

"The man in the black armour. I was spying on your meeting. She's not been taken to the capital. He's taken her away. I asked my father after they had left. Asked him how he could just sit and watch while she was taken away." Her eyes went vacant, as she slowly raised her hand to her cheek. "Never again," she whispered, almost to herself.

Gren seethed with rage, putting two and two together. He knew Lord Cunningham wasn't particularly enamoured towards his daughter, but he didn't think he was capable of striking her.

Roth cursed. He lowered his voice. "Look, child, I knew Lana's parents. I found their bodies. I was too late. I followed Lana's tracks which lead to the river. I assumed she'd been swept towards the capital. I didn't expect her to be picked up before the river forked." He turned to Gren. "For that, you and your family will forever have my gratitude." He looked Marissa in the eye. "Will your father know which direction they were headed? I can't afford to be wrong this time."

Marissa nodded, tears beginning to roll

down her face. "It sounded as though it was planned."

Roth bowed to her. "Thank you, my Lady," he said, heading towards Daltons Hill.

Before he could go, Gren grabbed his arm. "Roth, who is she to you?"

Roth stopped and patted Gren's shoulder. "I'm her godfather."

He took off at a run. They watched as he grew smaller down the road, eventually disappearing from view.

Gren put his arms around Marissa's shoulder. "Do you want to come back with me? Mother should have dinner ready, if the Lady of Daltons Hill wishes to banquet with simple farm folk."

She laughed amidst her tears, pushing him in the direction of home. "That will suit the Lady just fine."

~

Lord Cunningham cast an irritated glance towards the piles of documents strewn in front of him. There were so many, he could barely see the wood of the desk underneath. Every one of them would need his perusal and approval. The thought of sifting through the mess felt like a lead weight in his stomach.

He fumbled between the piles in search of his wine jug, eventually finding it and toppling some of the papers off the desk and onto the floor. He cursed in frustration, filling his goblet with his favourite dark claret.

It was late. His quarters were wreathed in shadow, the only light coming from the torch hanging on the wall above his head. He looked towards the window were the moon was visible in the clear night sky.

Deciding the correspondents could wait until morning, he called for the guard stationed on the other side of the door.

He didn't usually keep sentries directly outside his quarters. After the two guards he'd sent to escort that idiot farmer's boy had been found beaten and unconscious on the road earlier, he'd felt a little better to have an armed guard close by until the perpetrator could be found. The thought of this thug, still at large, made him feel uneasy.

He'd questioned his men as his physician had treated their wounds. A hooded man had taken them unawares and attacked them. They had been unable to get a look at the perpetrators face, as it was hidden beneath the hood of his robes.

Their looks of shame, as they told their sorry tale, had incensed him. He'd sent them home, docking their wages for two weeks. It would not do for his men to be bested by a mere vagrant.

But was it a mere vagrant? From what little description they had provided, the fact their attacker wore a robe made him think of Kerr, that arrogant Knight of the Hour. But he dismissed it. The Knight was so desperate to reach his godforsaken temple, he wouldn't have enough time to go there and come back.

So, who had it been?

He looked towards the door. Hadn't the guard heard him? He barked an order once more failing to hide the annoyance from his tone.

There was no reply.

Growling, he scraped the chair back and got up. He stormed to the door and swung it open in a fit of rage.

His guard lay on his side at his feet, his bottom lip was swollen and bloodied.

Before he could react, a hand grabbed him roughly by the collar, and pulled him back into the room. He was sent sprawling into his desk scattering his documents everywhere but the table. His wine jug tipped over, rolling off the desk and shattering against the cold stone floor. It spilled the rest of its contents over some of the papers, ruining them.

He heard the door close quietly behind him. He turned and felt his face grow pale as the blood drained from it. A hooded figure in front of his only escape, save for the window, but that wasn't really any option being six floors up.

The hooded man stood there tutting. Tutting in his own quarters, Cunningham couldn't believe the gall of the man.

"What a mess, my Lord. I assume those

are important documents," the hooded man asked, pointing to the floor.

Cunningham followed his gaze to the carnage on his floor, almost speechless with rage. "How dare you break into my keep. Assault my guard. There are several guards on this floor alone. One call from me and they will be here in an instant to cut you to pieces."

The hooded man chuckled. "Two at the top of the stairwell, four posted on each corner of the corridor." He inclined his head back, towards the door. "And your man out there. That's not including the four sentries posted on the floor below, and the five on the floor below that. I'm well aware of your soldiers, my Lord. I can say with certainty, they weren't aware of me. So, shout all you want, be my guest."

Cunningham did not doubt he was telling the truth. His confidence evaporated in an instant. He felt his bowels begin to weaken. "My men earlier, that was you?" he asked, knowing what the answer would be.

The hooded man nodded. "I felt inclined to help a poor boy being bullied by two of your finest, my Lord. Not a good representation of your noble self."

Cunningham was at a loss. He looked down at the shattered remnants of his wine jug the way a man dying of thirst would look at a mirage disappearing before his eyes. He was relieved to find his goblet had not been relieved of its contents. He grabbed it and drained it one draught.

The hooded man gestured towards the chair. "Please, my Lord. Take a seat. I have no wish to cause you any harm."

Cunningham's gaze flicked to his chair, then back at the door.

The hooded man followed his gaze. He flinched as the hooded man took a step forward, shaking his head. "That is, if you provide me with the information I seek. Time is of the importance, my Lord. I have already wasted the day, choosing the right opportunity to sneak into your keep so we can have this little chat. Believe me when I say I am in no mood for games."

The Lord's shoulders sagged as the last vestige of resistance vanished like smoke in the wind. He dragged himself around the table and dropped into the chair with an audible thump. He sighed. "What do you want to know?"

The hooded man took another step forward. "The girl? Who took her, and where did they go?"

Panic gripped him like a cold hand running down his spine. He couldn't tell him about the girl Argon took. If the captain found out he'd been betrayed, the consequences would be unthinkable.

He wondered how long it would be before one of his soldiers were found by his remaining security. He racked his brain on how to stall the imposing figure looming over him. But for how long? It could be minutes, for all he knew it could be hours. He couldn't fight his way past, he'd never been in a fight in his life. The hooded figure had rendered over a dozen of his best trained soldiers incapacitated without raising the alarm, he'd make mincemeat out of him.

He had to try. He had no other alternative. "Marissa? What do you want with my daughter?"

The hooded man slammed his fist down onto the table. Cunningham jumped, and to his shame, yelped in a high-pitched squeal. "Lana, Cunningham," the hooded man roared. "Lana. I'll ask one more time. If your stalling, then you're no use to me, which means there's nothing stopping me from throwing you out of that window." He leaned in closer, Cunningham backed against the back of the chair. He could feel beads of sweat beginning to run down his face. "I will turn the world upside down to find her. If you're games causes her anymore harm, I will return and burn this place to the ground with you in it."

Cunningham could feel his crotch grow warm as his bladder failed him. He closed his eyes and hoped it was just piss. "Argon," he blurted out. "Captain Argon. He took her, he didn't say where, believe me. He left with a dozen of my men. I saw them leave from the ramparts, heading west towards the mountains. What do you want with an orphan girl? She means nothing?"

He regretted the last words to spill from

his mouth as the hooded man leaned a little closer. He could feel himself being scrutinised for any signs of a lie. Though he couldn't see the man's eyes, his gaze felt like spiders crawling over his skin. He felt like vomiting. He could taste the bile in the back of his throat, and his mouth had begun to water.

"That is my concern," the hooded man growled, pulling back, and turning on his heels towards the door.

Cunningham breathed out, he hadn't even realised he'd been holding his breath.

The hooded man opened the door and stopped, glancing back at him. "Thank you, my Lord. I hope for your sake we never meet again."

Then he was gone, leaving Cunningham alone amongst the mess of paperwork, and the stale stench of urine. He lurched forward and vomited a mixture of bile, claret, and shame all over his desk.

~

Roth had already scaled the walls of the keep and travelled two hundred yards towards the forest before he heard the bells signalling alarm.

He smiled grimly, turning around. He could see more and more flickers of torchlight moving between the windows of the keep – presumably searching for him. The pompous Lord hadn't given him much to go on, but he'd been telling the truth, and it was better than nothing.

He just hoped it was enough to find Lana.

Epilogue

The palace courtyard was shrouded in darkness. Torches lined the walls, casting their light along the cobbled stone walkways as sentries patrolled the perimeters, razor-sharp pikes held high, in predictable intervals.

The rain had given the cobbles a film-like glisten, the shadows cast from the lemon trees, strewn around the grass courtyard, spread out like grasping claws.

The one known as the Wraith hugged the outer wall, hidden in shadow. It craned its long, horned neck back, as it watched two of the royal guards passing, oblivious, underneath. It licked its lips, almost failing to control the urge to leap down and rip the two men apart with its long black claws.

It rolled it's eyes in frustration, then cast its gaze further up the wall towards a flicker of light coming from the highest window. It smiled – or at least gave an expression of one with its cruel mouth.

It waited until the patrol passed, and disappeared around a corner. Not that it mattered if it was seen, being more than capable of silencing the guards before they'd opened their mouths.

It began to climb.

The tower would be impossible for a human to scale without the aid of their crude climbing tools. Their clumsy hands would struggle against the smooth stone. The Wraith climbed it as easily as it had walked to the foot of it.

It stopped and turned, looking out to the vast clearing that sat between the city walls and the great forest. Hundreds of tents almost covered the entire area. It could see the soldiers flitting in and around it like insects around a nest. Their primitive army looked ready for their march west.

It smiled and continued its ascent, drawing closer to the window. The sounds of gasps, and grunts grew louder. It slowly grabbed onto the window-ledge and raised its head over the top.

The Queen was writhing on top of a male in that idiotic mating ritual these pathetic creatures seemed obsessed with. The Wraith struggled to hold back a laugh at the scene before it. It was baffled how these beings had defeated its master centuries before, regardless of their magic knights from the now ruined temple.

It slid through the window, the rooms occupants oblivious, too embroiled in their coupling. The room was lit with only a few candles, the Wraith easily found a spot to conceal itself in.

It watched in detached interest as the Queen and her companion finished this ridiculous charade. It couldn't help but smile as the Queen arched her back, as her body shook with pleasure. The male made a grunting noise, and quivered himself, gripping the Queen's buttocks, as he spilled his seed in her.

The Wraith remained as still as a statue, waiting patiently.

~

Isabel gasped, and cried out as she climaxed. Skallen reciprocated with a growl. She felt the warmth of his seed as it spread through her loins.

She did enjoy his late-night visits. He was as virile as his brother was. They usually made quite a racket, but she wasn't worried who heard. No-one but her maids were allowed near her private chambers late at night, despite their insistence of at least one guard posted nearby. The fools knew nothing.

She rolled off Skallen and filled a goblet with wine. She drank deeply, she'd worked up quite a thirst. She turned to the King, laughing inwardly at the title. He was a puppet, he just didn't know it yet. Naïvely, he thought he was the architect of the current course of events.

He got up and began to dress. He was a lot less chatty than his brother, which she liked. They would wed next month as was tradition when a King died and his unwed brother ascended to the throne.

They'd kept their little late-night meetings a secret, as was appropriate. The mourning period for King Hal was almost at an end.

Besides, she was 'recovering' from her ordeal.

"Will the army be heading west soon, my King? she asked.

He nodded. "Within a matter of weeks. Lord Arnold will lead the initial expedition. I will lead the rest of our forces shortly behind him, after we've wed, of course. I should reach Daltons Hill by the time he reaches the mountain gate." He turned and made for the door. Before he left, he turned back to her. "Helven and King Richard will bow to my rule, and one King shall rule all the land for the first time in centuries, with you at my side as it's Queen."

She bowed as he closed the door, leaving her alone in her quarters. She blew out a breath and rolled her eyes. Gods he had the personality of a block of wood.

Hot from their lovemaking, she approached the window, the gentle breeze cool against her skin.

She looked out to the city and the army camped outside its walls, ready for war. Her city. Her army. She rested her arms on the ledge, and leant out. The rain pattered against her head. She raised her head up, letting the rain spray against her face.

She was suddenly startled, as something grabbed the back of her neck and pulled her back inside. She was whirled around violently. A dark shadow, with a long neck and cruel face stared at her as it gripped her by the throat and lifted her off the ground.

Fear rendered her speechless – that and the fact she couldn't speak or scream even if she wanted to, as a cold, clawed hand wrapped around her neck. Its face was alien, but it was also a face she recognised.

It was the Wraith.

The Wraith pulled her closer. Its breath made her want to vomit. "I see we're enjoying our new-found powers, Isabel," it rasped at her, throwing her onto the bed. She instinctively covered herself, knowing how ridiculous it was. The creature standing before her found her just as attractive as the bowl of fruit sitting in the corner, or the drapes hanging above the window.

"What news from your master? Is it time? As you can see, the army haven't left yet. They will be within a few weeks," she said, her voice shaking, and not from the sudden chill in the air.

The Wraith climbed onto the bed, and stood looming over her. It bent down and raised her head up to meet its gaze with one of its talons. She could feel it digging into her flesh, drawing a little blood. She'd seen its horrible face many times before, but it still made her want to scream her lungs raw.

"You have played your part well, child. The Fury will bless us with his presence soon," it whispered, almost tenderly – almost.

"And I will be rewarded for my loyalty. He said he would in my visions. You know this."

It nodded, smiling that gruesome grin. Its sharp teeth were pointed and crooked. "Proceed as planned. Make sure your puppet king sends his armies west. You will be rewarded soon."

She nodded. "Will you be staying in the capital? Is that wise? If you were discovered," she asked, nervously.

It laughed. A terrible noise that elicited anything but joy. "No, my child. You humans are such primitive beings. I will advise from a distance. Now sleep."

Before she could answer, it reached down and covered her face, cutting off her air supply. She grabbed at the claw, attempting to prise it from her mouth and nose. She thrashed and kicked as her vision began to grow blurry, eventually fading to black.

~

The Wraith watched with amusement as the Queen struggled in its grip, eventually her panicked thrashes slowed, then stopped altogether. It removed its hand and checked she was still breathing.

Satisfied the Queen would wake up with a sore head, and a tender jaw, it leapt off the bed, and loped over to the window. It looked up at the night sky and smiled, thinking of the bloodshed to come.

It began to speak the words of the prophesy. Words that held a promise to the realms of men, long overdue after centuries in exile.

"Soon the Fury will engulf this land in blood, and rule with fear made of iron."

Acknowledgements

I would first like to thank my wonderful wife, Karina. Who has encouraged me from the very beginning, when I decided to give writing a bash. She has had the patience of a saint, as I exposed her to my mad ravings on plot, characters, and general direction of the book. She read my earlier drafts, giving me feedback that was both honest and constructive. It wouldn't be the book it is without her.

I found as the book progressed, and the plot began to grow arms and legs, it helped I had people close to me I could rely on for constructive criticism and feedback. For that I would like to thank Jeanette, as without her guidance and experience (being a screenwriter herself), I probably would have missed certain elements of the book that needed attention.

I would also like to thank Nik from Book Beaver covers for the absolutely amazing cover art. For being patient with my input. Giving me suggestions on what would be the best way to have the cover designed. You gave me a front cover I love.

Thank you, Fraser, for sitting next to me over the months while I emptied my head of all my ideas in a vast tirade that may have seemed endless. Hopefully, now that it's finished you may get some peace… although work will commence soon on book two.